The Letterbox Man

I0633812

Laura May

chipmunkapublishing
the mental health publisher

Laura May

Published by
Chipmunkapublishing
PO Box 6872
Brentwood
Essex CM13 1ZT
United Kingdom

http://www.chipmunkapublishing.com

Edited by Aleks Lech

Chipmunkapublishing gratefully acknowledge the support of Arts Council England.

Dedication

For Mrs. Bickmore, as promised, the first one is
dedicated to you.

For Patricia Mole, a lady to the end. I miss you Nanny.

For my granddad, Brian Couzens,
because when you went I knew life was too short not to
write this book.

Laura May

Acknowledgements

Thanks to Chipmunka Publishing as always, for publishing something a bit different and letting me play with words the way I like to.

Thank you to Hazel Freemantle, who spent many nights nursing a drink with me as I tackled my writer's block, and who then became a friend for life.

Thank you to all the great people I met while researching this book in the village of Polruan, Cornwall, I will always think of you dearly.

Thank you to my great family, for all their love and support. Special thanks to my mum, without whom this book would be littered with spelling mistakes, and for always being my hero.

And of course, thank you to Brooke, my angel, for making me write the ending to this novel, even though I didn't want to let it go after such a glorious love affair.

Author Biography

Born in 1983, Laura May is the oldest of six children, and always felt a bit 'different'. In 2008, after ten years of being treated for a range of mental health issues, Laura was diagnosed with Bipolar Disorder, and subsequently discovered she also has Borderline Personality Disorder.

Over the past eleven years, Laura has experienced suicide attempts, psychotic episodes and several bouts of extreme depression and mania, all of which she has tackled through her creative writing.

Laura May now works within mental health marketing, and possesses a degree in English Literature from the University of Hull. Laura lives in Essex with her wife and their 'babies', the many cats and dogs.

'The Letterbox Man' is Laura's first novel. Find out more about Laura May at www.lauramay.org

Laura May

Prologue

Some say drowning is peaceful. It sweeps over you like a feeling I wouldn't feel now, like a memory of a better time. But waiting for the water, the beautiful, hopeless water of centuries, to take you; it must be torture. The longest moment of your life, waiting with a hope that the day will shine through, waiting for anything at all to break through the noise.

Falling in love must be like drowning, drowning in too many smiles and promises and knowing you might not make it out without breaking into pieces. Some say drowning is the best way to go. But once you go you're gone of course, forever lost in photographs and people's fragile minds, lost in the past. The past, that can never be regained, never be touched again with fingertips, never hope to be tasted once more.

For me, drowning seems so certain, so promised. In my deepest dreams, I know only the river will greet me, only the river will take me home to my heart again. I know the water will capture me; like a shard of glass, I will be worn away with time. With lost love. Breathing in so deep, I know I will embrace the waves, the salt, the air I cannot hold on to, I will fight and struggle at first, until all I want to do is nothing at all, all I want to think are empty thoughts, all I want to taste is my wet mouth filling with no more tomorrows. I know.

But I am not afraid. I am not unsure of my path, I know where it will lead, how I will be embraced once I'm gone, who I'm going to.

I know I will remember the best day, the lightest morning, the latest time I slept until, the streets wet and wonderful, your door with flaking paint, and the kisses I felt, like you meant them. I know. And nobody likes to live a life without feeling as though they learnt something, anything, to hold onto as their head goes under for the last time. And now I am ready. I am ready to go home. To my sweetest of loves.

Chapter One: Monday

Beth, aged 84

'No matter what you dooo, I only wanna be with yoooouuu'. I turn the radio down and Peter looks sideways at me. I wish he wouldn't, these roads are so narrow and difficult to master if you are not used to driving on them. Six hours of road we have covered, twisting and turning like a good plot, getting nearer and nearer to the village, to the beautiful river that shapes the people, to my past. It's so strange, being back here.

Polruan is such a beautiful village, with a Cornish heart and sunny summers, but even as we drive in I can feel the suffocation settling upon me, my breath catching in my old, rattling lungs. I can't quite believe the days have passed, despite me leaving. The gulls still cry, for a loss I don't know of, the storms still rage, although today is a beautiful sky. It seems so quiet here, so calm. How anyone can sleep in such silence is unimaginable, although once I must have slept soundly here. I must have.

Now I need sounds to rock me off to sleep, cars and sirens and life tapping against my window as I close my eyes. I guess I have just grown used to noise. Being back here is like bumping into an old sweetheart years after the tears have dried. When you look at them you can see them saying your name, see their lips moving, but you hear the ringing in your ears of the first kiss you shared, the first looks you stole.

I can see this village, and I will see the changes, the disappearance of the bakery and how weary my mothers' house has become, but all I can hear are the ghosts of my past moaning on the breeze and winking at me from behind clouds.

Her house looks much the same as when I left it, so many years ago, a lifetime ago. I have to adjust my glasses to read the sign by the door, even though I know what it says. My eyes, so old, how much they have seen and how little I still know. 'Welcome Home', the sign reads.

It's like turning around to another time, coming here. I feel ashamed to think that I didn't want to come back and sort out the house. After all, it can only stand here for so long, empty and grieving. A grown woman not being able to return to her home seems bizarre, but I just couldn't come here before now.

I thought my heart would be too old to take another break. I thought I would be too old to try again, to try and see this place without tears in my eyes and screams ringing in my ears. I am old, and it is time. Time to say goodbye to my nightmares and my memories, and goodbye to the smiles of my past as well, all the happy moments that filled my life when I was here. My old bones, worn with age and life, need to rest. They need to be home.

Despite fleeing this place so many years ago, and returning only a handful of times, it feels right to return now, to die in the same bed as my dear mother. It feels right to return to a blanket of comfort, to wrap my old life around me once more. It feels OK not to take the long way any more. It is time.

The village is old as well, older than I am. I catch glimpses of it before we reach the door, wrinkles spread out upon its streets. It is a dying place, without new birth but so beautiful in its decay. There are still the two pubs, boasting real ales and home-made food, and a couple of shops left. But the village of my childhood, the smell of freshly baked safety, no longer lingers in the air.

Somewhere in between I can feel him. He is still here, peaceful, content never to leave. I just want to taste his love, even after so many years: years I have filled with children and trips to markets and smiles from friends. It feels strange being here, it really does, but 'strange' doesn't even begin to encompass the raging that seems to flood my senses as soon as I step out of the car. As my foot touches the ground it is as though the earth shudders in recognition of my return. 'We have missed you' whisper the steps, 'you're back' creak the doors. Nearly eighty-five years of life, and still I am nervous of coming home.

Peter and I enter the house as though we are burglars, and for some reason we feel the need to whisper, even though the only people to hear us are long dead. I don't know why, but I have an uncontrollable urge to laugh out loud, and my high pitched giggling breaks the spell. Peter laughs too, richly, like his father. I find the meter and get the electricity going, and when I turn the radio on it seems almost rude, the happy carefree sounds of another world seeping into the four walls we stand within.

I stand alone in the centre of the small living room while Peter makes tea. The ceiling is low, scraping along the wall as though barely remaining aloof. The dust is everywhere, in the corners of the cabinets, sinking forever into the carpet, covering my heart with a layer of recollection. I think of the last summer my father came home, how his smile filled this tiny room and he hugged me to him. I remember the look my mother gave him the morning he left, almost as if she knew she would never see him after that day, never feel the unshaven roughness of him against her again. I remember thinking at the time that she didn't look sad though. She just looked tired.

I would like to lead you through the corridors of my childhood, inspect each room of the house while tugging at your hand, pulling you along through the debris of tangled lives. I would like to tell you all about the Christmas my mother got drunk and my father carried her up to bed as though she were a child. I would like to tell you about the day Kitty and I tried to open up the well at the top of the hill and I nearly fell in.

I would like you to walk beside me throughout the whole of my lost life, the nights I stayed up late and the mornings so beautiful I can't even remember the colours of the sky, the pavements that shone after the rain, the days I dreamt, the turnings I didn't take and wish I had. However, this tale is not of my childhood. It is about my love.

Peter comes in with steaming tea in dirty mugs, shaking me from my past again. I feel a little irritated that he is here, an alien presence within this house, this home, not even thought of when I inhabited this space. But that is why he insisted upon coming with me, to drag me away from anything painful, any thought that may give me that far-off look I sometimes get now. But I want to be alone right now, moving amongst the shadows of my youth, my childhood captured beneath the floorboards of this house, my home.

I survey the room, turning slowly. The door jamb where I hit my chin as a baby. I don't remember, but Mother would repeat over and over how my father had jumped out of his chair like the hero he was and swooped down to catch me. I can smell the freshness of the beautiful dresses my mother made for the rich ladies of the village. I see my mother and me sitting at the wonky table in the corner planning my wedding, my mother constantly getting lost in her own thoughts and me getting angry that she wasn't paying attention.

I know now how that is. I see Peter getting impatient with me as I gaze upon my past, laid before me like a sheet of paper, the lines smudged and vague with time. I put down my tea, and then we begin to clean, methodically, picking a room each, traitors to memory, wiping away a life with our damp cloths.

It's such a mess. The house seems bruised with all of her memories, all the dust of a lifetime. My mother was such a tidy woman, everything in its place. Somehow the years have paraded through the house, unsettling everything. I think of the pattern she began, and I am thankful I have no daughters to pass it on to. I want my children to live, not survive. I find the photograph when I'm clearing out her second bedroom. My room. Once upon a time, until I left her, all alone, to swallow her grief and redecorate. Until I ran away from my own life.

The photograph is of my wedding day. I have never seen it before, it must have been gobbled up with all the others. Joseph looks handsome, smiling into the camera, eyes glistening even in black and white. I am looking away to the right, looking serious. I wonder what I was thinking about. I always did look distracted in photographs. My mother would borrow the box brownie from the Spencers and would try again and again to capture me, but I'm not sure she ever did. 'Beth, look at me, not over there!' she would exclaim, click click click.

Peter is pottering about, I can feel his footsteps. Perhaps I should show him the picture, paint for him the man his father was. A kind, gentle man that loved me like he loved the sun, like he loved the sea. That is how I define him, in relation to me. How selfish, but that's the only way people know how to define others.

He finds me curled up on the single bed that creaks like my bones, clutching the photo and sobbing like a child. I suppose I'm like a child to him now. I've given them all my strength over the years, now they have to look after me in return. He eases the picture from my clenched fist, smooths out the crumpled face of his father. He smiles at me, looking like Joseph had the morning we met. He smiles and puts his hand on my arm, his eyes searching mine for an explanation, a reason I would cry. He has heard fragments of these stories so many times before, I have spun so many tales for my children, as all mothers do, but he wants to hear again the legend of a man he'll never touch, never know.

How do you paint such a man? Capture such a love? To fall in love once, hard and fast so that your blood rushes to your head, is no great feat. Anybody can fall in love once…it is so easy, falling into open arms. But twice? Perhaps a little more difficult. Maybe only I think this, because I know how hard it is. I've never asked anyone else. I have fallen in love twice. With the same man. The first time it was like chocolate melting in my mouth, warm, sharp. The second time it was as though my heart was whole, filled with so much more than I ever imagined. Filled with the Letterbox Man.

I realise Peter is still sitting on the bed beside me, looking at me openly, his face filled with concern and interest. He is such a good son, a little patronising of me, but indulgent. I am glad, suddenly, that he has come to Polruan. He has been denied its pleasures too long. I have held him at bay, it is time to let him come home. He has this river in his blood, he has the sea running through his veins, it is time he realised it. He is a Spencer. He has poetry nestled beneath his skin, a love to give to someone special that may not survive, laughter to sing, just as his father before him had so much to give to the world.

Eventually Peter goes, when I have stopped sobbing, but he leaves the door ajar as he goes downstairs. I know he is worried about me, they both are. They think I am having a breakdown; that I am caught up with too many ghosts. They didn't understand at first when I explained that I had to come here. James refused to come with us. I don't think he is ready, but I hope he will be soon, before it is too late. I understand. I do. But it is enough now. It is time to forgive the river, to let go of our anger. Peter was happy to join me, to escape his own life for a while. After all, he has no ghosts here, he has no memories of this tiny village and all the lives it holds. I am glad of this, in a way. It makes it a little easier.

I tidy my hair in the mirror of my mother's bedroom, and go downstairs. Peter is cleaning cupboards, scrubbing away at the old wood. He is whistling along with the radio, he doesn't notice me until I have been watching him for a while. He smiles up at me, that condescending smile he reserves for me whenever I get emotional. The way he holds onto me with his smile reminds me how old I am. I smile back. Time to get cleaning.

Chapter Two: 1937

Beth, aged 16

My Beth,
Are you 'my' Beth yet? In my heart I feel you there with
me, snuggled against my other loves, beating with me.
So I will say 'my' Beth for now, until you decide to leave
my heart, though I fear you never will. I fear that you will
reside there until even after it stops beating, so that I will
forget you are there. You will become part of me. And it
is this fear that assures me that yesterday was the
beginning of forever.

The beginning of many days that you will light for me,
that you will give me your smile, that I will want never to
end. Now that I have tasted you, felt the softness of your
eyes looking upon me, I will never want for anything
more. And so you are 'my' Beth.

I saw him once, before we even met. Mother had a
dress for Mrs Spencer, an exquisite, elegant green
dress of tulle that I touched whenever my mother looked
away. I had even helped on some of the stitching, so I
insisted on accompanying her to the White House. Just
being inside his large, noble house made me want to
share his life.

The house stood at the top of the hill, staring boldly out
at the sea below, beautiful and quiet and calm. As a
child I had dreamed of living in that house, of gliding
along its hallways, covered head to foot in the rich, soft
material that my mother used to make her dresses. I
was so nervous, entering through the side door
clutching tightly to her arm.

The Letterbox Man

I was fourteen, and already infatuated with the tall house and the dusty smell of the kitchen. Mrs Spencer had smiled at me, pretty herself then, and as she had left the room I had seen him through the door. It was like brushing my fingers against a soft skin. Just one second, imprinted on my mind, and completely forgotten as soon as I left, skipping merrily along with my mother as she jangled coins and promised fish for tea.

We met quite by accident, two years later, on one of those deliciously cold mornings that I love. The chill so crisp you wouldn't know it was in the air until it sneaks up behind you to catch in your throat. I heard him before I saw him. Heavy footsteps pounding behind me, snatched breath, urgent. Then he hit me. I have always insisted that Fate threw him against me, though of course it could have been ice. But Fate can be as cold and indiscriminate as ice. I didn't even recognise him as Joseph Spencer, the soft skinned wonder of my childhood that I had glimpsed in the White House.

That morning I didn't make it further than the crumpet shop on the corner of Fore Street. Instead of returning to sew with my mother I sat and drank weak tea and listened to the dreams of the man I was going to marry. It would be lovely to be able to look back and think that I knew Joseph was the man I was going to marry on that day, but I confess I didn't. I had no idea how hard I would fall, how violently I would need.

Dreams, so vivid and intense as they spilled out of the nervous boy before me, were catching. They clung onto me like spores, hooking themselves to my future. To wake, wanting the day to be over, and to fall asleep wishing the day would never end. If only everyone could have a day like that in their lives, a day that holds a beginning and an end and lets light in.

'I'm a writer you know, well, I write...does that mean I'm a writer?'
'Well, I suppose it does, yes'
'I'd hoped you say that...would you like to read some of my stuff?'
'Yes, I'd love to...'

He had been so unsure of himself, in such need of care and attention, in need of praise. I had always imagined, in my limited way, that anyone who had been to Oxford would be confident and secure. But he had played with his napkin, fiddled with his hair, looking up at me with those eyes that held a thousand stories, and he had been so unaware of his affect on me.

I want to know you. I want to know what makes your eyes crinkle, and what makes your heart stop, and what wakes you at night. You make my eyes crinkle. You make my heart stop. You wake me at night. That first letter held my heart like I never thought it would, broke boundaries I had never before ventured beyond. That first letter. I can't even explain it; it was the beginning of so many letters, letters that proved to be the glue of our love. Letters that never stopped arriving, letters that hurt and healed in equal measure. God, it was the beginning of so many letters.
So, our love began. Slowly at first, building and budding against the tide that we hoped would not engulf us. How does love begin? With a smile, drumming in your ears, too many words? Our love began with a day, with letters filled with too many words and hopes of so many smiles and the constant thud of my heart in my ears each time I saw him, each time I tasted him. Our love began, and I, foolishly, thought it would never end, thought his letters would take me through my life like whispers in my heart. Our love began.

Our stations in life, so very different, naturally caused a scandal in the village. You cannot convince the world that your love is the one that will transcend, that this is real and strong and will withstand the tears of difference. I was so scared he would not give it a chance, would not want my heart, although it could never belong to anyone else but him. But each day my mother would smile at me in the morning like she had smiled at my father before, as though she knew a secret about me that I had yet to discover.

Mother seemed so proud that I had captured the heart of Joseph Spencer, Oxford graduate and general 'nice boy'. Thinking back, it was only the grumbling rumbles of war that allowed us to marry. Without war, it would never have been permitted, so for that, I am thankful.

He smelt like Christmas. Chocolate and oranges and tobacco. He always had cold hands from being outside, I loved that about him. When he touched me it would shock my skin, the coldness, or maybe just his touch. Every time I saw him I couldn't stop my eyes tumbling down from his head to his toes. He was beautiful. His hair lay against his cheek, always falling across his face. He would hide behind it.

But it was his eyes, as blue as a river, that looked at me as though I were more than I ever thought I could be. That was his gift to me. He saw me, when nobody else did. He saw my hopes and my fears, and he enjoyed being part of both. His thoughts would graze mine, his voice would fill my head. We were so happy, doing nothing at all.

I wished for so many things when I met him. I wished I could paint, so I could paint him. I wished I could write, so I could speak to him the way he spoke to me. I wished I could sing, so he could hear my hopes springing into the air every time I saw him. I wished I could be worthy of him.

We fell in love so fast, so easily. Just looking at someone and feeling… well, just feeling. Feeling dizzy, full up, feeling hungry for just one more moment to be pressed into each day so you can stay together a little longer. I would starve myself of him for days, sure that this time I wouldn't need to see him again, just in case he didn't feel the same. But I always needed to see him again. And he always felt the same. *This is the best day I can ever remember. And the time on the clock when we realised it was so late. I'll remember that, and one day I will create a time just for us so that it will never be too late.* I divided my time then between seeing him and thinking of him.

I knew that I was his. Every time I saw him he made me want more. Love is so demanding, so selfish, especially young love, you need to fill it with such energy and you take all you can from it. That's what we did. If we spent an hour with each other I would demand another, always craving more of him. I was baffled by my own lack of control when we met. Suddenly it mattered what Joseph thought of me, it mattered that he understood. I had never cared too much for other people's opinions of me, but Joseph made me want approval. I wanted always to feel like his, to deserve him.

He shared his sea, his river, with me. We would sit for hours on the jetty, shivering and content and wanting nothing to ever change. It was these moments, filled with salty air and darkening skies, that sealed our fate. The sea created a life for us, joined us in silent appreciation. As our desire consumed us, the sea swallowed our doubts, our insecurities, and it breathed love into our looks and laughter into our smiles.

I remember the first morning that I awoke to his breath on my body. I stared at his back, at the mole on his right shoulder that was so perfect in its ugliness, at the nape of his neck, and I knew then that I wanted him all for myself, more than I had ever wanted anything. I wanted his teeth nibbling at my ear, I wanted his tongue flicking across my belly, I wanted his hands holding me.

We were so clumsy that night, knotted and chaotic in our passion, our legs snarled together, our hands fiercely tugging at each other's skin, our heads dizzy. I had wanted men, desired their rough hands against me, their sweet sonnets in my head, but he offered me more. He offered me the sea, the morning, a million tomorrows. Inside me, he filled me, with want and hope. And eventually, with love. He tasted so good.

'This almost makes it real, waking up with you,' he said as the sun shone in on that first morning. And he kissed me then, that way he had of not even touching my face, just leaning into me, learning the hollows of my mouth.

Long, hopeful months passed before Joseph proposed to me, and I stuttered like he had when we first met over my acceptance. Several months of broken sentences and hidden kisses outside my mother's house. I would watch him from her window, kicking the litter and muttering to himself. I forgot to notice the seasons, the changing colour of the leaves. Time dragged along the ground like a petulant child. The letters did not stop.

He wrote words that in my dizzy affection I believed were better than all I had ever read before. The young heart of a girl is as delicate as a feather, and like a feather my heart floated softly into his palm with those words. *I think I'm falling so in love with you I may never be the same again. You make me want to be a better person. You make me a better person when I'm with you.* My mother called him the Letterbox Man. She would smile when she heard the letterbox slam. It was almost as if she thought the letters were for her. Perhaps my father had written to her when they first met. I never asked.

It was the words that I fell in love with, if I am honest. Those hopeful, hopeless words that would caper about in my head until I could analyse them no more. He could never escape his thoughts, he let them bubble up and out of his mouth, out of his pen, whether they were loving, or hateful, or honest, he just let them spill over into the air, onto the page. His letters were so full, they were bursting as they slipped onto the mat. *Today I went over on the ferry to buy you flowers. But they were the wrong colour so I threw them into the river. I shouldn't have. They seemed so beautiful, sinking, I almost jumped in and retrieved them. So I'm sorry. I should have dived in for them. But I do love you.*

One page could hold so much. I would read them as I rushed up the stairs, so impatient. His letters were addictive then. Each held so many layers, I would imagine him returning and adding textures and moments and meaning to each page. His letters held his heart. In them he combined two loves. I think that's why he wrote so many.

When I held those letters, I never imagined we would ever argue, but of course we did. Our first argument was so silly. We always argued about silly little things, skirting anything that might divide us permanently. He had bought me a pair of mittens and I had told him they were too expensive. Such a silly thing to argue over, but we did. He became so angry with me. He always looked so lost in anger, he could never understand himself, and he always forgot his lines.

'Why the hell can't I buy you things Beth, everyone likes new things!'
'You don't need to buy me things.'
'But I want to, or don't you like them, or don't you like me?'
'You are being silly…of course I like them, and of course I like you, I just don't want you to waste your money on me.'
'How could anything for you ever be a waste?'
I remember crying, softly, like a wounded little bird, and he had bristled until he couldn't resist holding me any more and we had kissed, so hungry to make things right, make time go back again. He had crumbled, wanting me to soften and soothe.

I had thought, after that argument, that perhaps he wouldn't love me any more. He would see the real me, see that we were different. Perhaps he did, but he still loved me. Perhaps he knew that I loved the mittens, even though I was consumed with the guilt of owning such an extravagant item of clothing when all around me the world was falling down. I always felt so ungrateful then when we argued, as though I had no right to complain when things were so wrong. But everyone argues.

In the mornings I would slip from home and meet him in the alley, give him my smile and hope he knew I was his. I could never say the things he said, I could never see what he saw. He saw bright skies and knew himself to be right in his thoughts. He trusted himself, trusted his actions like someone ignorant of reality. I don't know why I fell in love with him. I cannot give the moment I began to see him a little clearer, I can't trap the second I knew under my thumb, I just fell into him, in love, out of youth.

There were so many things that were not right about him when we met. He was not who I wanted to fall in love with. He muttered to himself when he wrote. My mother loved this about him, but I hated it. I hated that he would spend so much time with this lover, this pleasure, when he was my only thought. He would use the same cup over and over again without rinsing it. He bought me balloons and forgot to buy milk, he liked the rain to soak into his coat, he liked the smell of me in the morning before I bathed, he liked that I bit my nails and tried to hide my hands from him.

But it was because of these things that I fell in love with him, not despite them. He saw so much more in me than anyone else ever had, he noticed the details. *Do you know that your smile is slightly crooked? You have a crooked smile, Missy, and I adore it. It is a chocolate smile, I could just eat it up!* When we first met he made me smile so much my jaw ached. I would forget the time and the rain and my wet feet. Although it seemed as though it was forever raining, I never bemoaned it then.

I welcomed his letters in those rainy days and sticky nights, waited foolishly for them, as though I thought they might stop appearing on the mat one day. Of course they didn't stop, not even when we were living together, in our small crumbly two-up two-down. It was three streets over from my mother's house.

I should have realised when we moved into that house that the soul of a poet is fundamentally different. I saw stained walls and a dirty fireplace. He saw rooms filled with light and love, a bed filled with passion, a hazy sea outside the window. What different sight we had. He saw a mirage of possibilities. *I have found the perfect home for us. We will be a family, and I will bring you breakfast in bed and hold you all through the nights. We can share our own world, yours and mine.*

I worried a little about money then, purely because I had never had money the way he had. Money just seemed to float in and out of our lives like coloured autumnal leaves, beautiful to look at but never making much difference to our path. *I will buy you a ring, my beautiful Angel, and with that ring we will be bound, forever. And when I am buying your ring I will smile at the clerk and tell him that I have found, among the pigeons, a dove of my very own, which will bring me peace.* We had matching rings, just plain gold. I say 'just' but what more could anyone ever want?

Our wedding was so simple, so easy, so expected. I held so much in my hands that day, a whole future for us to share. I would be Joseph's light, all he ever needed. The scandal of our union, the whispers of my ways, faded into the background that day. Even the imminent chaos of a predicted war that was rising around the village at the time could not thwart our happiness. I ignored the posters, ignored the leaflets banging through our letterbox, threw them carelessly aside and concentrated on his letters, his promises. He promised we would be safe, and I believed him.

Despite the warnings and the radio announcements, I honestly believed my little corner of the world would be left untouched, that my new husband would be safe in my arms. What did I care for fire precautions and blackouts while wrapped up in my new love? I didn't.

Joseph worried more than I did during those days, burying himself in pages of poetry and missing hours. But on our wedding day we were happy. The entire village was happy, enjoying the reminder that life continued, blossomed even in the darkness. The church was so full I thought it might burst, or that my heart might, as I walked up to Joseph. My mother had cried as Joseph's father had walked me down the aisle. I'm not sure if she was happy.

I couldn't quite believe it when our marriage began. Suddenly so many things changed. I was just a child really, clinging onto a vision of adulthood that had seemed so appealing in my daydreams. The strangest thing was not working. For the first few weeks I was at such a loss. I had lost my youth, my mother and gained a beautiful man that I did not know quite what to do with. But our marriage had begun. A marriage that would last only a handful of years really, but years filled with smiles.

He still wrote me a lot of letters from the jetty, even after we were married. *You are my sea. Beautiful depth and silent strength. Perhaps that is why you scare me sometimes. You are too strong, you can wash all the bad things in the world away until there are only smooth surfaces. And I could drown in you.* I always enjoyed living by the sea, but his love for her was raw, passionate, it consumed him.

When he first returned from Oxford, before we met, I think the sea had been his first love. The attraction between them had been instant. Later, like a child I would compete for his attention, keeping him tangled in hot sheets, snatching his time. After the first year of marriage I felt as though my two rivals, his pen and his sea, were old friends. I would chat to them, wave happily back as I walked along the shore on the way to my mother's.

Our house was so sweet, and it was filled with a love that in my youth I thought unique. Before James was born the second bedroom was his study. He never wrote in there though. He preferred sitting in the garden, looking out at his sea as he smoked one cigarette after another, flicking them over the wall. I would scold him about that. I wish I hadn't now. There were a lot of little things that I would scold him for, just so he knew I could.

Our life together was a beautiful picture, painted with smiles, but it did have shades and smudges as well. We would argue and shout and make up, as all people do. But I always fell in love with him all over again when I watched him write. The expressions that paraded across his face, it was as though he was making love to the very page. Such gentle concentration. He never made it hard for me to love him.

Chapter Three: Tuesday

Beth, aged 84

My Beth,
When I die I want you never to visit me. I only say this because Sam's brother died the other week, and Sam has spent the last few days hurrying to and from the churchyard like a man possessed. It got me thinking that I would not like you to be like that if I ever died. You shouldn't visit me, if you can help it. I will be smiling in your heart, drying your tears with my fingertips. You will not need to ever leave the house to see me; I will be there, shadowing you forever. I promise, my Beth.

Peter and I begin walking to the church, up the hill that as a child I thought nothing of climbing. Now my legs are so unsteady. But I insisted we go. I wanted to see Joseph's grave, and my mother's grave. I have not seen his stone for nearly twenty years, the last time I came here. The church seems new, shiny almost, as we approach, even though I know it is so much older than the teeth sitting unevenly in my head.

The afternoon sun holds a little warmth, and I can feel the pin from my poppy scratching at my skin beneath my coat. Peter has fallen in love with the village, the sea, just as his father did when he first came home from university. I can't seem to stop the spell that it is weaving upon him, although I am subtly trying to discourage any attachment. I couldn't lose another love to this place.

Out of breath and red in the face we reach the church. Peter goes inside to find out where the stones are, but I know. My feet trace a path straight to my husband, guided by a memory. Someone has put fresh daffodils in the container beside his stone. Who here has cared for his grave? I feel as though nobody should remember him but me, nobody has the right to love him but me. It's selfish, but I feel violated by this kind gesture.

It is odd to think that once, long ago, our love could not last a couple of years without shattering. Now our love has lasted almost a lifetime, spanned two children and many moments with and without each other.

I want to lie down on the damp grass, dig my fingers into the earth, touch him again, but I resist the pull. The daffodils seem so bright in the shade of the trees, shining for me alone. It is sharp, the pain I feel in my breast as I remember my loss, but it's only fleeting. It passes, like it always does. You never get over it, you just learn, each day, to cope. To push down the dull, aching loss that threatens you. You just cope.

I don't hear Peter, but I sense him coming towards me. With him is a beautiful woman, quite striking with her red hair in the sun.
'Mother, this is Sarah.' His voice seems so deep. As a child his voice was always so high, too sweet, a bit like James.

'Hello dear.' I barely recognise the whisper that escapes my lips.
'Sarah looks after the graveyard.'
'I hope you don't mind the daffodils, it just gets so dreary here without any colour...' her voice is like cream, thick with a Cornish accent that I no longer own. I am overwhelmed with a desire to speak in such rich tones again, as I did as a young girl. Would Joseph recognise the twang of my voice now, the hints and shades of the East End that have invaded it?

I turn back to my husband's stone, the words I chose for him so many years ago, without really thinking, without understanding what they meant. It is so very old, this stone, even the dates are fading, but I can still make out the words.

Take yourself away, be gone,
Tomorrow we will smile for you,
Go, have peace,
And tomorrow we will be with you.
Joseph William Spencer
You are my sea. Beautiful depth and silent strength

The words were from a poem Joseph wrote, while he was away, when his friend was killed. I don't know why I picked that poem, I never liked it. It was so forgiving, letting go. I was always selfish in that way, I never wanted people to leave me.

'I love the words.' Sarah is talking to me, but I'm not really listening. I am thinking that she is too beautiful to be here, surrounded by the deaths of a hundred years, the end of so many heroes. Her hair is too red, it belongs to life, not death. Peter comes forward, kisses the stone, and then takes my arm to leads me away. I don't want to go, don't want to leave my handsome, funny husband again, but I let him gently steer me towards my mother's grave.

I look up at him and I can see the concern etched on his face. He is thinking this was not a good idea, that I will become 'emotional', as he says, as though that is a bad thing to be, a weak female thing to be. As we near my mother's grave I register more daffodils, a couple of days old, needing some rain, but still glorious. Peter and Sarah leave me alone, and I chat to my mother as if she were sitting beside me. I have missed her, I realise quite suddenly.

I sit, pattering on about the boys to my mother who has been dead for more years of my life than she was alive. I find this very sad. I look down at the river rushing along below. It is high tide. The water is violent against its banks, the colours deep and dirty against the reflected skies.

I have not returned to this village for many years, and yet I feel a rivalry with this river flaring under my skin, this beautiful, never ageing element that has filled so many lives, when I have filled only a few. When Joseph died I moved away from all of this, severed so many tight bonds.

I took my angry, bruised James, and my new-born Peter, and I fled from all the pain of memories that shouldn't have inhabited my mind. I shouldn't have had the memory of Joseph's death within my heart at such a young age. If anything, he should have remembered my death, when he was an old, grey man, his life led. I shouldn't have had the memory of giving birth without my husband waiting expectantly outside the whitewashed door of our bedroom. I shouldn't have attended his mother's funeral without him, seen his father's loss without Joseph there to help me prop him up. I needed help from him, I shouldn't have been so alone.

This place does something to me, something deep inside. It stirs so many memories that should no longer be vivid. In a way it is something wonderful. I feel as though I am being thrown against my life, battered against my past, and it feels refreshing, although it hurts. It hurts like hell. But most things worth any salt do. They sting.

I think of this as I chat to my mother absently, tell her about James' retirement, about his pretty wife who is always late, the garden of his house that she has created for him, filled with daffodils for him, because she cannot have children. I sit on the damp grass and I tell her about Peter's unease, how like Joseph he is in so many ways, how he refuses to remarry despite it being five years since June's death. And she listens.

Finally, I let Peter take me back. I still can't think of it as home, although it was once the only home I knew. I can feel Joseph singing to me on the wind as we descend the hill, I can feel him in my heart. Peter chatters away gaily, as though we had been to a carnival or a fair for the day, not to visit his father's grave. However, I cannot be angry with him. He is too good. I could never be angry with him, even when he was a child.

Finally we reach the old house. Inside the air is swirling about the living room, catching the light, dust motes dancing in the colours of another dying day. Peter puts on the stove and I sit down, take up my knitting and listen to him talk to James on the phone in the kitchen.

'Yes, yes, everything's fine…yes, a bit of a mess, but nothing Ma and I can't sort out between us…yeah, we went this afternoon.'
His voice drops to a hush and I can't be bothered to listen any more. So what if I refused to leave for two hours? What is two hours compared to a lifetime without him? I nearly said that to Peter but I bit back my words before I hurt him. It is not fair to hurt him.

I can't walk too far now, so we settle in the top pub for a drink after we have eaten dinner. I need a sherry after getting 'emotional' today. Or so Peter says. I am not going to argue with him, he is like the parent now with me the helpless dependent. I need him more than he needs me now, as is natural.

I study him as he leans against the bar, chatting with the pretty woman who is serving him with a smile. Such a handsome man. All mothers think their sons are handsome, but mine actually are. He is an old man himself now, I suppose. So many years of love, and then they grow up. He is so very like his father, he smiles in the same awkward way. He has the same restless nature, the same hunger for life that Joseph possessed. One day he will make another beautiful woman very unhappy, no doubt.

I think of the girl, Sarah. She is hardly a girl, she must be over forty. But that hair, so young. Peter seems quite taken with her, thinks she is very intelligent. I doubt her mind is all he admires, but I just smile and nod as he chats away, as though he has known her for an eternity, not an hour.

'Be careful Peter' I mutter as I sip my sherry.

'What do you mean, Mother, she was perfectly nice to you...' He tries to continue but I wave his words away with my hand. I know I'm in trouble already if he calls me 'Mother'.

'Mermaids are beautiful Peter, but many men drown for them.'

'Oh for goodness sake Mother, she's hardly a...'

I stop listening to his protests. I blank out the sound of his voice and look at the old pictures lining the walls of the pub. Some are of people I know, I realise. They have ended up black and white and hanging on walls as all people eventually do, becoming shadows. Peter is still babbling on about judging books by covers or some such nonsense. I smile at him.

'You know my hair was that colour when I was her age.'
He stops talking.

How I loved the hill when I was a child. Sliding down it in the coldest winters, feeling the crunch of snow beneath my boots and letting the frost seep under my skin. Now I can barely drag myself back up it. As soon as we reach the house I beg exhaustion and make my way up the wooden hill to bed. It is strange sleeping in my mother's bed. The bed I was born in, the room I first screamed into. I turn and stare out of the window at the river purring below, running nowhere.

How can I still miss him this much? I wrap my own arms around me, feel the smooth texture of my stomach beneath the rough tips of my fingers. I wonder if he would still want me, with laughter lines circling my eyes and my hands twisted beneath a blanket of arthritis. I think of what he may be like. His beautiful eyes would deepen, his skin would wind itself around his changing bones, he would still mutter to himself as he made my breakfast. I think of this as I fall asleep, and wait for another day without him.

Chapter Four: 1938

Beth, aged 18

My Beth,
I think your mother likes me, you know. She has taken to calling me 'The Letterbox Man', did she tell you that? You have her smile, you know, Beth. When she glances at me from around the table I can see it playing upon her lips, and I see it on you as well when you wake in the morning. It is a beautiful smile. I hope our daughters borrow it from you as well, to make the men smile back at them. It is a gift.

I should have realised that such happiness always has a price. But I chose to ignore my mother's worried looks, and the radio bleating constantly in Mrs Spencer's kitchen as though it would deliver an answer. I knew, in my heart, what was coming. We all did. My mother would stare at Joseph as he sat at her table, drinking tea and smiling at her jokes.
'You are a good boy, Joseph' she would sigh.
'And you are a good girl, Anne' he would smile back at her.

In those early days of the war, she would often giggle like a teenager with Joseph, then smile sadly at him. She knew he would be taken from me, she knew the price I would have to pay for him. She never said anything to me though, she just encouraged me to stock up on food and candles and kisses. Which I did, willingly, thinking it all a game. And then as my stomach grew, my ignorance grew, blotting out the world and its shadows.

When I realised I was pregnant I could not wait to tell Joseph. But I did wait, a couple of days. I would smile at him in a knowing way, and he would question me with his eyes as though he knew I was hiding a beautiful secret that would complete us. I had expected him to jump up and down with excitement when I told him, but he didn't. He was stunned in a way I had never witnessed before. His eyes caught such a look of bafflement, he could not believe it.

For a man that created such amazing poems, he couldn't understand how he had created something so simple and precious. He placed his hands on my belly, perhaps expecting to feel through me, into my womb, feel the life he had contributed to. For a moment I had been terrified that he didn't want it. Then he smiled.

That smile stayed with me for a long time, following me, infectious. He would love me softly each night, as though he wanted to climb inside me and feel the warm breath of our child against his skin. *I love you more with two hearts beating within you, more than I ever thought I could love. I will love you more in a year's time no doubt, but at the moment I feel as though my hopes are so high your kiss might kill me, your smile might just make my heart stop. Are you as excited as I am?*

We would smile constantly in those days, secure in the knowledge that we needed nothing else but each other and the baby within me. As I grew bigger so did our smile, spreading across our lives, to all that met us, all that knew us.

His face changed, the day I told him I was pregnant. The lines smoothed, the creases retreated a little, and he looked younger, as though the new life inside me was the beginning of his own life as well.

We were like children then, playing in our very own doll's house. We would look at one another across the room and whisper 'I Love You' into each breath at night. Our heads were bubbling with all the moments we had shared so far, and all the memories we could create in the future. The feel of moss, warm and damp, soaking into my coat as he pressed me up against the wall of my mother's back yard. The smell of ink on his fingers, staining my body as he touched me. My head swam with caught kisses in those early days. The mornings then would beckon us from our beds, entreating us out into the world.

Our house was not far from the quay, just a little way up the hill, and we would run down it to feel the spray on our cheeks, the wind stinging our skin and each other's laughter singing in our ears. He loved his sea. She was like a mistress, demanding and moody, but always providing something I couldn't give him. He would love her for hours, pushing his feet through the surface, enjoying the cold tingle as she caressed between his toes.

I often caught my mother watching him from her kitchen window.
'Your Letterbox Man is muttering to himself down there again'
'I know, he's writing Mother... It's very important that he has time to write...'
'Perhaps it is a love letter for you.'
'Perhaps it is,' I would reply, knowing it was.

When watching Joseph Mother would sigh wistfully as she plunged her red hands into the soapy sink. I was so defensive of him then, always explaining his writing to people when he wouldn't, always lending it value and importance, as though it was bigger than us.

Mother would reprimand me; 'You are too fierce when it comes to that boy…relax, nobody is attacking him.'
'I know, it's just his writing is very important to him, so it's important to me as well.'
'Yes, dear, I can see that.'
She would smile tightly at me and pretend she understood. Maybe she did.

Throughout my pregnancy Joseph wrote so much, so many articles and pieces he didn't really want to write so that we could buy little bonnets and little booties. But he wrote to me as well, and this he enjoyed more than anything. *If our child is a daughter she will be so beautiful I will have to lock her in a tower until I can find a man who will love her much as me, more than me. And if our child is a son he will be so strong not even the sea will be able to break him, and only love will be able to weaken him. I hope I can love our child as much as I love you.*

He could never stop himself from thinking, could never hold his thoughts at bay, they were always playing within the walls of his mind. I loved this about him. I hoped our child would be like him, intelligent and gentle and filled with something that I could never hold on to. I hoped that our son would be handsome and strong. I knew, even before James was born, that a boy sat cradled against my heart. This knowledge filled me with pride, a wife's pride at being able to give my husband a son. It would be my greatest gift to Joseph.

Even with the world looking over our shoulders we smiled, looking forward to the arrival of joy. The evening that James was born so many pieces of our lives fitted together. As soon as I saw him my mind blocked out any struggle or pain that he had caused in the five hours I had been willing him into the world. Joseph chose the name James. He sighed it as soon as he saw him, and I knew it was OK, it was right. It was his younger brother's name, although I didn't think of this at the time. Perhaps my son looked like James the very evening he was born, but I didn't see the likeness until a few years later when I knew Joseph's brother a little better, could recognise his looks a little easier. But I was glad to borrow his name. It suited my son.

How could something so tiny cause so much light and fear, change so many days and nights? Joseph was so natural with him, so easy with him. I think at first I resented this in him, his ability to hold our baby and know he was going to be fine. I worried constantly about James in the first few months, never wanting to leave him. How Joseph put up with me I'll never know, but he gently guided me into motherhood, pushed me a little into my new life. His words helped me so much then. But I never said thank you. Nobody ever does, really. How can you thank someone for giving you your life?

After James was born I thought our happiness would never end, it would engulf us and hold us tightly together. A complete circle. A mother, a father, and a child, complete. But although I was content to let the days fall to the wayside and pretend evil didn't exist, Joseph kept one eye on the world, always wary of change and conscious of the part he must play. I ignored everything but my beautiful men, forgot to worry about anything other than feeding times and tired nights. I only wish that was all we would have to worry about.

Chapter Five: Wednesday

Beth, aged 84

Peter has fallen in love with the village over and over again each morning. I can see the light dancing in his eyes as he looks upon the river each day. From every angle you can still find the river. It breathes life into the village, you can feel it pulsing, constant, below the earth. I have been dreaming of Joseph since we got here, and I'm losing track of the days, caught up in the nights that I know will bring him back to me. It's quite lovely though, having him so close to me after being away for so long. I find I am actually quite enjoying travelling along the back streets of my mind.

Peter has been gently hinting since our feet touched this soil, and I finally feel like giving in today. We are going on the ferry to Fowey. He knows it will be hard for me, treading onto the river, swallowing my fears of its hidden depths and powers, but I am determined to do it, finally. I'm tired of this distance, this lack of courage that has been preventing me for so long.

It's ironic to think that once I was such a strong swimmer, confidence filling each of my strokes as I swam across every summer with the other children. It's amazing what you lose with age, that ideal of infallibility that each child holds in its heart. I no longer possess the conviction that I will live forever. I know I am old, my hands are tired, my eyes no longer see as well as they used to. I can feel my body longing to give up, struggling each day to rise and carry on. But I carry on.

I remember wandering the quay in Fowey with Kitty, comparing hair styles and greedily swallowing fish and chips, the salt stinging our lips and the vinegar making our eyes water. The smell of the men as they got off their boats, laughing deeply and winking at us openly as only grown men did. I remember a day, in the middle of a windy autumn, when my scarf blew away from me on the ferry home. I had laughed along with the other passengers at the time, but cried late into that night, remembering the softness of its lilac fur. How strange to remember that now.

It's windy today, God is huffing and puffing at my hat and I pull my coat a little tighter as we walk down the hill. Peter is excited, childlike in his eagerness to get on the boat. Sometimes I regret leaving here, taking the sea and the sky away from him when he could have had a very happy childhood, a safe childhood, like I did. But for all I took from him, and from James, I gave them something to replace it. I gave them an extra kiss each night and an extra smile each morning. It was all I had left to give.

I stand on the steps and watch the boat drawing in, watch the elegant old man tie the ropes securely with such practised ease. The people getting off, cheeks rosy and full of the wind that whips their scarves in their faces. Peter gets on first, helps me down the step and seats me on the bench. I close my eyes tightly and the man looks at Peter in recognition of my fear. I can feel their smiles being exchanged in the air between them above my head. I reach over the edge of the boat, let my fingers brush the surface of the river. It feels as though Joseph is licking between my fingers, lapping against me.

It's hard to hate this river when I had loved it for so long, adored and feared it for so long. Like a spurned beau I feel resentful, angry, but somehow desperate to make amends. I forgave her a long time ago, knew that she needed Joseph more than I did, but I am still afraid of her powers. The river has retained a beauty and elegance that I lost years ago with my youth. She holds a quiet grace that I wish I possessed.

Peter is watching me. I can feel the concern buried in his look without turning around. But I'm OK. Now that I am actually in the boat I don't even want to get off, I just want to stay like this, with the cold water biting my fingertips and the wind singing for me, remembering. I am old now, my memories are jumbled up like old scarves, but they are colourful enough for me.

Round here, he is always on my mind. I feel, when I get on the boat, like I am walking on water, like I am walking all over Joseph. My heart is thumping for the entire fifteen minutes that it takes to reach Fowey. I can feel a smile spreading across my lips. Perhaps I'm smiling because I'm nervous, I'm not sure. Perhaps I'm smiling because Joseph is kissing me on the breeze. I open my eyes, gaze about, allow myself the pleasure of a glimpse of open sea when we are about half way across.

I let my eyes rest on the castle, and a flash of memory catches in my mind; Joseph and I sitting out on the rocks at the castle, with two days facing us. I close my eyes, see the sun setting in a roar of colour on one side, and the moon waking up over the hills on the other side. I shake my head and the memory spreads out, gets thinner, and finally washes away. Peter is staring at me when I open my eyes.

As we reach Fowey my arm brushes against that of the old man driving the ferry. He smiles at me, like an old friend, and I wonder briefly if I used to know him. The smell of salt and vinegar assaults the senses as Peter helps me up the slippery steps. My wedding ring flashes in the sun as I pull on my gloves. I notice how old my hands look, like the hands of a weathered lady.

We wander around aimlessly before finding a pub for lunch. So many things have changed, while staying the same. The food is good, hot as it burns my tongue, and it tastes like home. I allow myself a sherry, smiling at Peter's badly disguised shock. After all, it is only lunchtime. The dim light of the pub is soothing after the glare of the sun, and I feel content, sitting here listening to Peter babble on about goodness knows what. He is going out with Sarah, and her flaming red hair, tonight. It seems this place holds more enchantments that I first anticipated.

I can smell fish here in Fowey. It hits you whenever you breathe in too deeply. Fish, the smell of my youth, emerging out of the past like a forgotten friend. When we leave the pub I insist on walking to the church. We sit on a bench and I gaze up at the clock, watching time tick, feeling the years fall away. I wish now that Joseph and I hadn't been married in this church. It looks too young to hold such memories. I wish we had been married on the river, joined together on the water. Then perhaps it would have held us tightly together instead of pulling us, tearing us, apart.

Trying to catch hold of him in my mind I sit looking at the beautiful, grand, formidable church. Peter is restless beside me, eager to talk, fill the air with words, to mask unsaid thoughts. Eventually he stands and brushes down his trousers. He is going to the shop for cigarettes, he will return for me. It's so strange to think that my son knows me so well, he knows he is losing me to the past, he knows that I am slowly saying goodbye to the church and to him too, in a way. Poor Peter and James. One day they too will say goodbye to everything they once loved, and hello to something else.

I sit here, surrounded by this green day and I know I am dying. Not in a transient way, like everyone knows that one day, in the future, their lives will fall away from them. In an immediate way. I know, in my core, that I have only really returned to this beautiful, magical corner of the Earth to say goodbye. Goodbye to all that moulded me, and hello once again to my Joseph, hello to my letters.

I am afraid, of course. I am not a fearless woman, I am not brave or courageous. I am timorous, uncertain, like a young girl. I am unsure whether I will recognise him again after so many years. I am scared that I am wrong, and I will not go to him, I'm scared that I will spend another eternity searching for him.

My fear makes me want to do silly little things. I want to eat too much ice cream, so that my head freezes. I want to swim in the river again. I want to walk to the peak, and re-live my memories until my eyes finally close. I am very afraid, I know I will miss my boys so much and I know they will miss me.

But I am an old woman. And age outweighs fear. I have lived so long, so many years, and as I sit in this churchyard gazing upon the beauty of a church that has united so many people and torn so many hearts, I am thankful for all I have been given. For all the letters I have ever received. I see Peter out of the corner of my eye, and urge my old bones to stand once more.

Chapter Six: 1940

Beth, aged 20

My Beth,
Tomorrow will be just fine. I promise you, I will be home sooner than you know. And when I get back I will smile down at your beautiful face, and kiss you once for each moment I have been gone, then I will kiss you each moment I breathe for the rest of my life. And while I am away I will kiss each morning, thinking of you. I will think of the feel of your eyelashes as they brush against my skin when you open your eyes each day. I will think of the colour that rushes to your face whenever I embarrass you. And I will be living in your letters.

The sea was angry on the morning that he left. I understood why. How could he leave her, abandon the one constant in his life? However, the sea forgave him for a little while when he returned. She let him take comfort in her again.

James was so young when he left, so I think that made it harder for him. I prayed then, that the man I had fallen in love with was dishonest and cruel and selfish and cowardly. I prayed so hard for him to be changed. Just so I could keep him. But he remained the man I had married, the man I had allowed inside me. I knew that he would prove to be every bit the man I thought he was.

It was the most terrifying moment of my life, that day he went to war. I would like to think that it was the moment I realised nothing would ever be OK again. But you never realise anything in a moment. We fell, not in love this time, but into a deep hole.

He went in as a Captain, and came home a mess. A Major, but a mess nevertheless, torn apart not only by shells but also by shock. I knew that it was all wrong, I knew it would happen, even before he left me. We walked to the quay together that morning, James pushed out in front of us. Perhaps we thought we could hide behind his innocence, his faith in simple days.

Joseph tried to smile for him every time he opened his eyes at us for confirmation that we were still there. I saw the hare before James did. It was peeking out at us from the side of the house as we closed the gate. James giggled hysterically at the sight of it, scaring it away. I knew then that Joseph shouldn't go, that the sea would swallow him, unable to forgive him.

I knew, in my heart, that we should turn straight around and huddle safe and warm in our house until the war was over. As soon as we reached the quay I saw my mother, chatting quietly with Joseph's parents, and when she looked up at me coming down the hill I knew that she had seen the hare too. Her eyes whispered all the warnings of a thousand years, that so many women had whispered to men over the years.

But I didn't tell Joseph not to go. I never told him that I had seen the hare. It was bad enough that he had to leave, without the knowledge that he would not return. I didn't know then that he would come home once again before the sea seduced him. Afterwards, I almost wished he hadn't come home.

I saw my mother trying to hide her fears behind her pride. I saw his parents, beaming inside their fine clothes. But the image that haunted me was the colour of the sea. The sun seemed to have dipped himself into the river, pouring all the colours of every fire into the gentling lapping waves that nuzzled the sand. It was so cool, that day. I remember feeling cool inside my clothes, wishing the sun were higher, smiling down on me, not looking up at me from the river. It was as though the war itself had seeped into the river, had strangled the blues and greens and browns that I knew so well. I don't think, even now, I can see past that colour when I think of his river.

When Joseph left he took my hopes with him, stealing them without me even noticing. He took so many things with him, his promises, his words, and my smile. After a few weeks the house no longer smelt of him, there were no cigarettes lacing the ashtrays, no apple core discarded on the kitchen table. And I tried so hard to remember which parts of him I hadn't kissed, to remember the taste of him. I tried. But he fell away, stumbled to the back of my mind and the corner of my heart.

The day he left me, left his son, I thought I would love him forever. I never imagined that I would fall out of love with him, that I would hate his letters and hope for wrong things. I so wanted to be in love with him when he came home. I just wasn't.

I wish now that we had made love the night before he left me, left us. Perhaps it would have sealed us together, stopped us falling apart. But I wouldn't let him be gentle, wouldn't let him love me softly. He seemed to understand my enmity, seemed to forgive my vicious hunger as I tore at his skin with my teeth and clawed at his back with my fury. He let me be savage, he let me take away the sentiment and the care from his touch, let me strip his caresses of their tenderness.

It was as though he expected my rage, as though he felt he deserved it. He let me hurt him, let me punish him in the only way I knew how, by refusing to let him be mild. He was such a naturally gentle man, such a good lover in his careful way. I wish now that I had let him love me slowly, so that it had never ended. I wish I had held him, rocked him to sleep, let him cry. But I didn't.

I remember the day before, my mother mentioned that perhaps he should leave his ring at home, so that it was safe. He had looked so lost when she said that, I had to touch his sleeve. He had looked at my hand, on his arm, and he had smiled up at me. He wore the ring the next day when he left, with a parting half-smile and a face filled with youthful hope.
I think it shocked him that he was actually a man, going off to war to fight for freedom and justice and all the other sentiments. His expression was the same as the first time he saw James. I couldn't understand how he accepted his fate, I was so angry at the world's indifference. I forgot, when he had left, that he hadn't wanted to go away, he hadn't signed up for the horrors of war, they had been thrust under his nose in a formal request. He had not asked for his fate, but I forgot this.

He had looked at me as though he'd forgotten my name that morning, he seemed so bewildered, in a way he was already absent.
'You'll be home in no time.'
'I know, I know…I will write to you, I promise.'
'Don't you worry about me…just…be safe.'
'I love you.'
'I know.'
He smelt so fresh and cold as I sighed my tears into his collar. I think James was a little scared of him as he stared up at him and accepted his kisses and booming

words of comfort. He must have looked so tall to James. He looked so small to me.

Why hadn't I told him I loved him? I didn't run after him, I didn't cry and scream at him to just stay a second longer, to wrap me up in his heart so he wouldn't forget me and be lonely. I let him get further and further away, until I couldn't see him any more.

He stepped onto the boat and turned to wave, and I knew then, maybe, that things would change. The sea cried for him as I did, two white tears screaming across the waves behind the boat. I felt then what I later recognised as utter fear. The terror that filled me when I thought I would lose him was so great, it was greater than my fear over James when he was born.

I missed him so much at first, I could barely breathe without him. I missed him like one misses a light breeze. You don't realise how much you need the touch of it against your life until you feel it again after a heavy rain or a close summer. I missed his voice, telling me not to pull at my hair, I missed his hands cupping my breasts, I missed his feet, cold against mine as he climbed into bed.

It's strange what you miss. I didn't miss all the beautiful words he gave me, these I held firmly locked away in my heart. Instead I missed having someone to argue with, someone to blame for the rain or not having any fresh fruit. He was so good at absorbing my bad moods, he would let me drop all my annoyances and moans into his lap without question, and his smile would make everything OK again. I missed him so much.

I dreamt of him for the first few weeks. It was always the same, a bird's eye view of his boat getting further and further away. Further away from me, standing all alone on the quay watching the river ripple at his departure, the breeze sighing with sympathy at my loss.

At first I took comfort in these dreams. Just being able to see his face each night as it got smaller and smaller was bliss. I was just so hungry for a sense of him. But the dreams soon became draining, wrenching my strength as I fought to hold onto the memory, the colour of his eyes, the warm smell of his breath. And the rain didn't help, forever beating against my window, demanding acknowledgement. The rain didn't help me at all.

Chapter Seven: Thursday

Beth, aged 84

It's unbelievably cold today. I feel it as soon as I wake up, and I try keeping my eyes shut tightly against the day, but in vain. The day will begin with or without me, so I decide to get up. The chill sits in my hands, edging around them until I'm so cold my teeth chatter, even the false ones. But I am determined to go today.

I have been meaning to wander down there since I arrived, and today I have persuaded Peter to bring along Sarah, the wonderful fiery redhead who seems to be occupying his mind at the moment. I'm sure she has explored the castle many times as a child herself, but Peter never did, and it's about time he learnt how to explore.

I can hear him whistling as he packs up flasks of the strong, hot coffee that I enjoy so much. Finally, after several glances in the mirror, he is ready, and we set off, slowly but surely. Sarah awaits us at the old bakery, and it's almost as though I can smell the redness of her hair. I envy her the colour; it was once mine. Like a child I want it back. Or perhaps I just want my youth back, I want to look at someone the way she looks at Peter.

We wind our way through the village, passing grand houses painted royal colours, and tiny cottages pushed together as though to crouch from the wind. As we head towards the castle I keep seizing glimpses of the river below us, between each house. It is as though it's following us.

We reach the decaying castle and I breathe in deeply. Only one deep breath and I can smell Joseph smoking beside me, I can hear the day ending all around us, I can taste the salty river in my mouth beside his kisses.

Sarah and Peter break the spell with their exaggerated appreciation of what must be to them merely a shell of a building. I smile up the crumbling stairs at Joseph as he darts in and out of the window casements, smiling boyishly as I giggle and sigh in mock fear. I smile at Peter and see his father in his features, see the charm that is obviously captivating Sarah.

This castle is nothing to Peter, it holds no lost summers for him. But I can see he is enchanted, more by my stories than by the actual physical building. We climb down a little onto the rocks, stand at the mouth of the river, looking in both directions. One way are the villages, and the lives of so many people; the other way is the wide open expanse of the sea, stretching forever, trying to touch the sky.

Finally we get out the flasks and sit awkwardly against a wall of the castle. I tell them of the time Kitty and I came crabbing here and Kitty fell in the river. We were in so much trouble for being soaked when we finally returned home. I tell them of the time I ran away here when I was very young, taking only an apple and my sewing kit, how my mother had found me curled up asleep inside the castle and carried me home without even waking me.

Some memories are private though. I don't tell them of the times I came here looking out to sea for my father, for months and months after he disappeared. I don't tell them of the time Joseph and I curled up under the stars in this castle and made love. These are my memories; I don't want to share them, to make them in any way common.

Sarah stares wild eyed throughout my tales, not quite believing me I fear, but enjoying each twist all the same. I have decided that I like her. She looks at me like a person, not like I am an eccentric old dear who has lost her marbles. I can see Peter enjoys thinking of how I must have been before he knew me, but soon he becomes more interested in climbing the rocks.

They leave me with my memories and climb out as far as they can. I watch Peter trying to keep his balance and Sarah laughing loudly, with her head thrown back. She is very beautiful. She has small laughter lines around her eyes that lend her a kind look.

I am glad we came here, to the castle. Only in Cornwall will you find a castle this beautiful, that retains such elegance and hides such atmosphere. I wander about inside the castle. There is no roof, the sky smiles down on me and I remember how much Joseph enjoyed writing here, getting dirty sitting on the floor and caring little for the fading light.

I never usually came with him, not during the day. He enjoyed being alone here, but I always enjoyed being here with him or Kitty. I always felt lonely here without him. I don't feel lonely now though, I just feel a little sad that Joseph isn't here to see his castle still standing proudly against the rough weather and careless time.

The last time Joseph came here was a little before he died. We all came, together, as a family. Joseph had bewitched James with tales of mermaids and shipwrecks and fantasy sea creatures of all shapes and sizes. It had been a cold day, but beautiful.

They had bounded up the steps of the castle and ran around play fighting until all I could hear were their cries and excited screams. Joseph had such an imagination, he could become a warrior, a pirate, a great sailor or explorer. I could only ever be me. I think that's what he liked most about me.

Exhausted and happy, they had slumped on the blanket beside me, and while James had slept cradled into me, Joseph had read to me, softly, without nervousness. He had whispered the words into my ears until I had dozed off happy.

I realise I am dozing now, remembering. The day is winding down, we have eaten and smiled and Sarah is gently shaking me awake to the evening. I stand, slowly, old and tired but content, and Peter begins to pack away everything. What a pleasant day, I think, as I look out.

Once again, it is like looking out on two different days. The moon is low, on my right, above the hills, and the villages are beginning to tire. On my left the sun is setting in a blaze of glory upon the sea, and a thousand brilliant colours are staining the water. It reminds me of another day I once loved. It is time to head back to the cottage and make tea.

Sarah accompanies us up the hill, and I hurry into the house with a wave to let her and Peter say goodbye. I lean against the door and listen to them, but it is made of such thick wood I can hardly hear a thing. I jump back as Peter pushes against it. He smiles at me knowingly as he closes it behind him.
'What do you think about staying on for another week, Ma?' he asks casually, once we are sat at the table with steaming tea. I smile at his attempt to appear as though he only just thought of the idea.

'There really is quite a lot we should do to this place if you want to sell it.' Peter says later, hopeful. I just nod, and smile. And so it is settled. I am not in any hurry to return to London. It does not hold the glamour and brightness that it once did for me. I find that I do not miss the Thames the way I missed the river here for so long. When I first moved to London the Thames provided such comfort, changing and moulding her moods to mine as only water can, but for all her beauty she is not my river, she is not mine. I am glad to be here, beside my river. Our river.

I decide to cook dinner for a change, and head off with scarf tightly wound about my head to the shop that sits snugly half way down the hill to pick up supplies. Peter protests in vain for a moment, then continues reading his paper. The day is ending and I wonder fleetingly whether the shop is closed.

However, inside it is warm and a handsome old woman is chatting to the girl behind the counter. I gather what I need in a plastic basket. While I am feeling the peppers I hear a voice that sounds so familiar I drop the pepper without realising. At first I think the voice is in my head, then I see the man buying tobacco.

His voice is like Joseph's, so rich and sweet, barely audible above the radio bleating away on the counter. I hurry to the front of the shop but he is pushing open the door before I reach him. I shake free the feeling that I know him, that I must have known him in another life, that his voice feels so close. I return to the peppers and forget all about it.

After dinner Peter decides to head out to the pub for a drink, but I decline his offer to join him and opt for a hot bath instead. I am so tired after walking to the castle today, after seeing so many ghosts running through its ruins. I need to wash away all the dust and the thoughts of the day.

I sink into the bath and let the water run along the creases of my skin. The heat makes me sleepy for a moment. I relax and let myself think over the day. I remember briefly the voice in the shop. When I left the shop I saw him edging up the hill in front of me, way in front of me. Perhaps I should have called out to him, asked him who he was, how he dared to have stolen Joseph's voice. But I didn't. I let him go. With this thought chasing me I get out of the bath, my fingers wrinkled from the water and my bones soothed.

Finally, I get into bed. This whole week has been so tiring, not in a bad way, but tiring nonetheless. I am exhausted as I lay my head on the pillow and close my eyes. Such a long day, such a long week, and not over yet. I am happy though, lying here in my mother's bed, I feel safe for the first time in ages. I feel as though everything is in its rightful place, me included. I sleep, and hope that I will forget to dream for once. It will be a relief not to dream of Joseph. I am too tired now.

Chapter Eight: 1943

Beth, aged 23

My Beth,
We arrived this morning, as the birds cried to the day as though nothing was wrong, and we have been so busy, it is only now, in the glimmer of a candle, that I have time to write these words to you. I should have made time earlier, but my men needed to be relieved, they were so tired. I miss you, Beth. I miss James as well...I only hope he never sees through his eyes what I have seen through mine. I feel as though I have many sons here, they are so young and scared, you could barely call them men. I'm trying my best, but I fear that my best will not be good enough.

One of them was killed last night, on the way here, and I can still hear him in my head. His name was Jack. He had a sweet face, kind eyes. I made them carry his body for miles, all night, so we could bury him here, alongside others from other places who didn't make it. I shouldn't have. It slowed us down and tired them out. But I could not leave him. There is a new light of respect in their eyes when they look at me now. But I don't deserve it. I only made them carry him for my own selfish reasons. I couldn't bear to leave him there, alone. That's all. I miss you.

He had been gone for nearly two months when the first letter arrived. For nearly two months I had woken up, holding on to that precious moment each day before I remembered he wasn't there. But then the letters came fast and hard, like heady first love. Different stamps, different dates, different worlds.

I sometimes wished he wouldn't write to me. *When I close my eyes at night it is too dark to sleep. I am learning to sleep with my eyes open. I hope nobody sees me and thinks I am dead.* I would keep the letters in the second drawer for weeks, saving them up, opening them at night alone as though they were a dirty secret.

Every time I did this I regretted it. The words would gush over the pages, rapid and illegible in their hurry to escape from their own descriptions, flooding my night. They would sit in my stomach, nestled against my fear and worries. *I am thinking of your beautiful face each day. I see you everywhere. Sometimes I can smell you.* But I could never throw them away. The need to read them was too great, the need to reassure myself that I was sharing in his experience, his terrible nights.

Some of the things he wrote during those two years he would never have said if he were home. *Sometimes I wish I had never met you. Every time I think of you it hurts.* Later, when he came home, we never mentioned the letters, the words he had written. To say out loud all those words would have taken a lifetime. We had already lost one of those. *Remember that day when I bought you home the lilies. And you said lilies were for death. I ignored you all night. I'm sorry.*

Some of the letters were brutally honest. *Sometimes I wish I was hurt, then I could come home. But danger seems to dance just out of the corner of my eye. I can feel it, but it never faces me. I know I sound ungrateful, sorry.* He apologised so much in his letters, for his own feelings, for the lost years with his son, for the world's ways and the fact that it kept on spinning.

It infuriated me that he apologised for being brave and human and courageous, when so many others never knew these qualities. Who the hell did he think he was? Offering too many explanations for other people's actions. *I keep igniting this hope that I will see you again. Some days, and every night, it is the only thing that keeps me going. Other days it strangles me with the impossibility of ever holding your smile in my eyes again.*

Suddenly the smallest moments became important, in his letters. He wrote so many, I nearly drowned in them. Each argument we had ever shared in our beautiful house became a crime, something to apologise for. Each morning he had forgotten to kiss me became a violation, something to torture himself with in these weakest nights.

Remember your mother's birthday tea, and I had mentioned drowning. I didn't mean to say that. It was stupid of me. His letters were so dense, so weighed down with reasons for the way he was. Perhaps he forgot, in the dark days, that those were the reasons I loved him. *I don't feel noble or right. I feel wrong in everything I do. The ground is so cold and hard that we can hardly dig to bury the dead. But we must bury them, or our hearts will become cold and hard as well.*

I knew that my letters held no emotion, no light for him. I knew they didn't, although I think he appreciated my effort. I have never been a great writer...I am too guarded. When I should have written to him about how much I missed him, how much I loved him, I didn't. I hid in the weather and James, like a coward. *It took so long for the water to get hot this morning, and this, more than anything, bothers me. When you come home you will have to check the boiler.*

Visiting the White House, I would be gazing at his mother, half listening to her voice that was so rich, and I would suddenly think of something good to write to him, but when I sat down at night to compose my letters all the words in the world seemed so inadequate. How do you convey that pain? The way the postman can make you freeze and melt into a puddle of tears in the hallway when he passes your door. The answer is you don't.

It's too difficult to hold your feelings beside your thoughts, there's not enough room for both, they are too raw. *James sang last week at school, and he hasn't stopped since! He has a high, sweet voice, like sunshine. He is missing you.* I should have said 'I miss you'. I should have scribbled it over and over again until I couldn't see the words. But I didn't. I filled my poor letters with what I thought would make him smile to himself, despite himself. I only hope they did.

Some of the women in the village envied their husbands. I never envied mine. I never envied his time away from a warm bed, his adventures. *Sometimes it's so loud I can't hear myself think. But it's worse when it is silent. Then my thoughts will not stop screaming.* I missed him, but I also enjoyed sitting alone with James and telling him fairy tales about his father. Filling his head with fanciful images of a tall man that could deliver a new world. I would read his letters to James, who would look at me in wonder, perhaps wondering how he would ever live up to a man who wrote such words, even though they were such simple words. *Be good for Mama. She is your angel, and she will keep you safe while I'm away.*

Mother would visit us in our crumbling little home, sit for hours with James and tell him legends of his grandfather, of his days at sea, the storms he had tamed and the mermaids he had swam with. Her head still jerked up as letters fell onto the mat, her smile held such sorrow. Perhaps she thought the sea would write to her one day and tell her where her husband was.

I envied my mother, not knowing the fate of her beloved. I wished that I didn't know. She saw it in me, my resentment, as I slipped further and further away from my heart. She feared; feared that I would one day become her, that I would wake up one day and not know where my husband had gone. I felt so ashamed of wanting something to happen. When Kitty received the news that her husband had died I was so jealous, so selfishly jealous. Her worrying would stop, she could now grieve and move on. I wanted so much to move on from my own harassed thoughts, my own lack of control.

So many things nearly broke me in those first few months without him. The world was spinning so fast then, changing so quickly, each day bringing new troops into the village, each night filled with new sounds, new thunderous explosions. I was no longer a girl, I was a woman, a wife, who had to protect her son at all costs and could not protect her husband at any cost. Every time I broke, cried, I felt so stupid at my weakness.

I remember ripping up all the flowers. James had stood, sombrely witnessing the destruction I was ravishing upon our small garden. He had cried when I'd said the daffodils had to go too.
'You're a stupid Mummy, I hate you'
'I know that, but we need to grow our own vegetables now James'
'But the daffies always wave at me Mummy'
With that he had sobbed his heart out for the friendly flowers that lay torn in my hands. I had gathered him up and promised to grow some more when Daddy came

home. He hadn't even answered me, couldn't bear to speak to me, he just sobbed and sobbed.

Within hours he had forgotten that he hated me and was singing his latest song to me as I put the daffodils into a vase and placed them on the kitchen table. I didn't deserve to be forgiven. I should not have pulled all the stems of our lives up, should not have torn so many coloured petals apart.

But eventually, there were happy days, pleasure in a bright morning or a smile from James. Quite simply, I learnt to live without Joseph. I fought it for so long, crushing the beginnings of any smiles before they sprang to my lips, consciously avoiding any social occasions, hiding in the cool, refreshing silence of the church.

But finally I had had enough. I had to dust off my heart and start living a life, filled with my handsome son and my caring mother and my patient friends, not filled with a man that was not even there. At the time I felt as though I had I lost so many days thinking about him, trying desperately to remember his favourite book or what food he hated, trying to erect an image of him in my mind to cherish. Finally, I needed to breathe a little easier and see what I had right there, right now.

I began to see the seconds of each day, to move a little out of my own head and smell the scents of the world. And I found they smelt good, they tasted of hope. James and I would sing together, while cooking the dinner, and he would seem so happy to have me. I wish I could look back on that time and offer myself a reason for my forgetfulness. I wished Joseph had hit me, bruised me, hurt me, then I could have hated him, people would have looked at me with pity and understanding when he returned, I would have been able to forgive myself for pushing him out of our lives.

I wish that I had met someone, a cocky American, a sexy stranger to fill my head with silly notions and my nights with dirty, sexy, shameful fumbling. But Joseph never hurt me, he only ever loved me, it was all he knew. And I never met someone else, never felt the soft fluttering of a new love enter my heart, never felt someone else's tongue pushing in my mouth. I just forgot how Joseph's love felt, that's all.

Days were so lazy, even happy then. People seemed bound together, united in their efforts to compete against the darkness that was devouring their sons and husbands and heroes. When the school was hit by the plane, the village rallied in a way I had never seen before. I felt useful, felt like I was helping, almost working again like I had with my mother before I married.

Joseph had not seen the scattered bricks of hope that littered the streets when that stupid German had crashed into our school. He had not seen the fear in every mother's eyes as we rummaged through the debris, searching for anything, anyone, and hoping that we wouldn't find a shirt or a shoe or a hand peeking through the rubble. He didn't know the utter joy that everyone felt when we realised nobody was hurt, the laughter that we tried so hard to stifle but couldn't, the release we so urgently needed as we all drifted back to our homes down the hill.

I could never tell him these things, I wanted the experiences to be all mine. Even later, when I began to get scared that the war would never end, and I would try so hard to stop James from crying, until he forgot how to, it felt safe with the arms of the village around us. We would sit huddled together, a little cold, a little scared, and tell stories and drink warm beer and pretend that everything would be OK.

In those days of war Mother would hold James to her securely, he would fall asleep in her arms, and I would feel as protected as he did just by knowing she was close by. It was terrifying, but when each morning shone through the window you felt so alive, there only by the grace of God. The reality that continued to crash down around my ears made me stop daydreaming, stop hoping for Joseph to come home. I didn't have time to hope for him, I needed to concentrate on James and me. Like silk stockings, hope is a luxury war doesn't allow.

Chapter Nine: Friday

Beth, aged 84

There is always someone you know, in Polruan. Everywhere you turn there is a familiar face, a knowing smile, a gossiping housewife at her window. It is so small that it cannot really exist in any other way. Since we arrived I have seen people that I vaguely remember from my childhood. Peter is amazed at the tightness of this community, how they steer one another through the storms as though they are all on board the same mighty ship. It is so different from everything he has ever known. But I find, surprisingly, that I have missed the suffocating warmth of this place over the years.

We are supposed to be leaving on Sunday, returning to London, although Peter has suggested we stay. I don't want to go, I want to live out the rest of my days here, I realise with a jolt. I'm surprised. I find myself walking past our house, the house that brought James and Peter into this world, I find myself wanting to roam its rooms and touch the grass of its garden.

I sold the little house when I left, and a deep regret is seeping into my bones, a regret that I haven't acknowledged for years. I also want to stay in my mother's house. It has stood empty for so long, I want to fill it with laughter again before I no longer can.

Peter, too, is keen to stay on. He has become joined at the hip with the beautiful Sarah, the scarlet mermaid. I must admit I am becoming used to the idea of her, she is sweet, and she quite obviously likes my boy. We are going to lunch with her today.

I tie up my hair and sit waiting for Peter to come downstairs so that we can go. I can hear the house creaking as he walks about, and I remember the sounds from my childhood. This house hasn't changed. The sewing machine still holds pride of place in the sitting room, shadowed only slightly by the photograph of my father frowning at me from above the fireplace. Peter makes a grand entrance, finally, swirling about like a schoolgirl, pouting at me, smiling like Joseph. I smile back, and enjoy his happiness. It is refreshing.

As we walk into the pub I smell cigar smoke, the beer soaked carpet, and I relax. This is home, in a way, this is comforting. Sarah is sitting at a table by the fire, reflecting the flames. A pretty voice is coming from the hidden speakers, the radio, but apart from that it is quiet in the pub. Only a few men stand at the bar, sipping from their own mugs, flirting with the barmaid and the time.

Peter orders our food at the bar. My eyes follow him and I notice an old, handsome man smiling nervously at me, apparently recognising me. For a flicker of a second I think he is Joseph, hope beyond the possible that he is here, that he has been waiting for me to come home all these years. I shake the thought away, and the man rises and asks to join us. Despite my own shock, the look on Peter's face makes me laugh and I realise who this man is.

It is Joseph's younger brother.
I know without asking.
I can almost taste the familiarity in my mouth.

'Beth?' he asks hesitantly.

I just beam up into his face. He looks so like Joseph it is breathtaking. He puts his drink on the table and looks at Peter, studies him openly, without embarrassment.

'James? Peter?'
The words are like a physical blow to Peter, and I sense him retreat into himself instantly, in his way. But he smiles at the old man, keen to humour him.
'I'm sorry, but I'm not sure we've met before' he says, confidently.
'Sorry, sorry, I'm J-J-James. James S-S-Spencer.'

Peter stares at him in shock, then looks to me for reassurance, for confirmation. But I can't stop smiling at this stranger from my past, this man who was once just a small boy on the edge of my vision, a briefly annoying child. For every second that I stare at him Peter and Sarah become more and more uncomfortable, increasingly unsure of what is happening at this small table in this tiny village in this beautiful corner of the world.

It's amazing how time skips into a new day, how two people, so unfamiliar, yet so connected, can collide. A small miracle, these days, that souls can push against each other in such a way, for memories to unite, for the world to witness. I am captured in this moment, drowning, as I am aware of the smells and sounds and the metallic taste of recognition in my mouth. My mouth, too dry to speak. With a whisper in my heart, I remember a morning too long ago, James licking a spoon after I had baked in our kitchen, his hair in his eyes. I shake my head to clear the image.

Eventually I nod, begin to talk to James, begin to explain to Peter that this is his father's younger brother. He was just a child when I left, when I ran away from everything

I had ever known and loved. It never occurred to me he would still be alive, that he would still be here, living out his life. It is amazing how like Joseph he is.

I am momentarily thankful that Peter never knew his father. This would surely be too painful for him if he had. Then I banish the thought. It is not painful for me. I soak up his voice and his mannerisms and the soft tobacco smell of his coat as though I am drinking in each likeness. He explains, slowly, his life. He hints gently that he has tried to find us over the years, that he has tried to make contact. The last time he saw me was at his mother's funeral, but he had not approached me.
'You looked so lost at the funeral, I didn't want to upset you' he explains.
I am simply stunned. I don't want to break into his soft voice, but there are so many things I find I want to ask him, about his family, about his existence. However, he senses this and leads us down the path of his life willingly.

I notice, every now and again, that Peter and Sarah are as enthralled as I am.
He still lives in the big White House that his parents shared, and it seems he loves it as much as they did, as much as I did when I first stole into it as a child. He has been married, and has four children, all of which have moved away from Polruan. His wife passed away two years ago. He talks of this quickly, rushes through his narrative, giving us no personal details of her, simply saying she's gone. I understand this.

It is fascinating to watch him smoking and talking before me. I have to remind myself to keep listening and not let myself get lost in my own memories. After the initial shock, Peter seems content to listen all day to this wondrous man who can provide such a wealth of memories of his father, and I am happy. Sarah seems captivated, and this warms me to her.

I am astounded by the chance of the whole encounter, how Fate has thrown him before me, this memory come to life before my very eyes. Suddenly here is a being who has lost what I have lost, a being who remembers different things about Joseph. He touches on the subject softly, as though he is afraid I will recoil from the pain of mentioning Joseph, but with a little encouragement from me he begins to light his memories.

James remembers Joseph leaving home when he was very young, leaving him his favourite book as a memento. I never knew Joseph did this. I forgot, at the time, that Joseph was also leaving his family for the war, I was so consumed with my own loss. He remembers, with a shy smile, how we had named our own son after him, and how upset he had been with us for stealing his name. I gulp in all this, it's as though I am thirsty for all the details.

James sings his stories and I realise hours have passed. The ashtray is full of cigarettes and our glasses have long stood empty. I am tired, worn out by all the excitement, and I think it is time to go. James seems disappointed, but accepts my excuses and promises to see him again before we leave. His eyes are a very touching shade of blue and as we say our goodbyes in the chilly evening air outside the pub I can barely tear myself away from him.

It feels as though he is the last person left alive that shares my past, my youth, my first love. I don't want James to leave my sight in case he is a mirage, a figment of my imagination that I have created to compensate for all the ghosts I keep seeing here. I think he can see from my face that I'm reluctant to let him slip through my fingers, and we arrange to meet the next day. I'm satisfied with this, and let Peter lead me up the hill, away from James Spencer.

It is late now, and I climb into bed. The sheets are cool upon my skin, the pillow relents against my head, and I close my eyes, hoping for sleep. I do not want to think about today, I don't want to think about James. I admit to myself that he is quite beautiful, in a soft, smudged way. I remind myself that he is not Joseph, he is not a young man in love, he is an old man waiting to die like me, just trying to get through each day without incident.

Something happened today. Something happened inside me, something snapped. I realise that I want. As old as I am, I still want. I want someone to talk to, to pat affectionately whenever I need to feel the touch of another warm body. I want someone to let me be selfish, someone to indulge me. I am lonely. And I am scared.

I have had too many chances to be happy that I have ignored in my grief, perhaps more chances than anyone deserves. But when James smiled at me today I felt something stir. I felt an instant affection for him. I push the thought from my mind, let images of Joseph's smiling face circle in my head and try to focus on these. I feel guilty. How absurd, feeling guilty after all these years. I am an old woman, I shouldn't be thinking like a teenager. Finally, sleep releases me from these thoughts.

Chapter Ten: 1944

Beth, aged 24

Joseph wasn't a saint. He was a good man, good in his heart, but not a saint. He wasn't infallible. He forgot anniversaries and slammed doors and smashed glasses like everyone else. He sat writing when he should have been reading the face of his wife, he danced as though he knew how, he sang out of tune and loudly, like his voice belonged to someone else. He complimented the wrong things, he smoked in the bedroom. He was not a perfect being, like so many people thought he was when he came home. How dare he come home and be perfect, when I had stayed at home, created our home, without him.

I hadn't heard from him in three weeks, but this had become normal by then. He had been moving all over the place, and hadn't had many chances to write. The letter seemed so shocking, so simple. *I'm coming home, my Beth.* I couldn't quite digest it at first, the panic rose in my throat so quickly I nearly fainted.

I had choked back disappointment and relief all at once, knowing I should want this so much with all my heart, but never allowing myself to expect it, never allowing myself to imagine the moment when those words would fall across a page and give me all I never thought I wanted.

When he came back I expected him to be broken. I expected a spectre of the man I married, a shell of all I knew and loved. But, surprisingly, he wasn't broken. It was so much worse than that. He was fixed. Each shattered fragment of his soul had been glued back together.

He had fixed himself so well that it took me longer than it should have to notice the cracks. At first I noticed the surface differences. But the cracks of his heart, the thin, invisible lines that had etched themselves beneath his skin, these took me a while. His smile still shone, though it never reached his eyes.

I almost didn't forgive him for being fixed. I had hoped to make up for all the injustice of the world, I had hoped that I could mend him with my own hands. I wanted the glory to be mine as well as his. I wanted him to acknowledge that he couldn't mend without me, even if he did this silently in thankful smiles and grateful embraces.

Like a child I believed that my warm skin could heat him, that my moist lips could hold him, lock him in. It was so much worse that he didn't realise this, did not knowingly fix himself. How can you hate someone who hates himself?

I knew, when he returned, that he had seen the horrors of faces too young, heard the whimpering misery of grown men, but knowing this did not stop me punishing him. I had also seen things too, things I never should have. I had heard things I did not ever want to hear again.
I had huddled among people I had known all my life, begging James to stop sobbing, as the darkness inched its way into every crevice of my mind. I had held him too tightly, throughout the lost years, like every other mother in England, and I had cried silently for the hearts that were broken each morning when the light came, and the post with it.

I had held Kitty so close when she found out her husband had been killed. I dried her tears and taught her to feel again. While my husband fought for his country I fought for the sanity of all the wives left behind. And Joseph could never see that, although he tried, I know he did.

It seemed, when he came home, that all our memories were divided, we didn't share any. I couldn't help damning this country that had taken my husband and trained him to kill. A country that sent sons away with their smiles and failed to make sure they had them when they returned. We didn't share enough memories to just slide back into love, I had seen too many things while never seeing what he saw.

I learnt to press my feelings against my breast. I had seen the river so full of boats you could walk from one side to the other, board to board. I had heard the school explode in the cold glint of another day, seen the bruised edges of what held all our precious little ones each day. I had smelt the breath of all the many children evacuated from Plymouth, eyes scared and faces too pale. But Joseph had seen so much more, and I didn't know what to do with him.

It took so much of my love to see him again when he returned. Despite myself, I had forgotten his smile, and the songs he sang, and the way his skin whispered against my thighs in the mornings. I suppose I thought he would never return. We knew, when it was announced on the radio, that he would have to go, go away from me, go to a war we didn't want.

Selfishly I thought only of my loss, my own inability to make the situation any better, my own bound hands. I thought nothing initially of his family, of his son, of what they may lose if they lost him, but only of my breaking heart. I could feel it thundering in my ears, all the moments we had wasted arguing or shouting or not telling one another that we loved. I love you, I would whisper to him. But he couldn't hear me any more. Maybe I should have screamed it.

I wanted to run away and hide with him, just the two of us, create a world of our own where nothing could touch me but him, nothing could hurt me but him. I remember his wan face, and the determined glimmer behind his eyes that I loved and feared. Suddenly five minutes of his love was not enough, I wanted forever, I wanted eternity, I wanted to keep him. I did not want to share him with the sea or the sky or the fresh air.

I felt so ashamed for not being in love with him when he came home. I loved him, a love that stayed below the surface and spoke only at night, but I was not 'in love' with him any longer, as they say. I had fallen past love on my way down, and had forgotten to clutch onto it with both hands. I had no right to fall out of love with him, I had no grounds to feel that way, but I did nevertheless. Who was I to feel that way? He had been away, he had missed all the comforts of a home and a family and a woman, whereas I had been kept safe in his letters and in his heart.

Perhaps it was natural to feel distant at first. He returned a stranger, with a darkness in his eyes that flamed only when he wrote, never when he held me. Perhaps I wanted him to be angry with me, to hate me for not being a stronger woman, for not writing each word that entered my head, for not telling him every day that I wanted him and needed him, that I breathed him. But he didn't hate me.

He made me into something I wasn't before. He made me stop wanting, stop hoping. Somewhere in those two years when he was absent I stopped missing him, stopped cherishing my thoughts of him. But for him, all through the terrible war, I held so much promise. So much more. *Today I saw a daffodil, the first of the spring. You are my daffodil, you are light and bright even when you are looking down. And when you turn to face the sun you shine. I miss that.*

Joseph's days were so blank, so empty, he had to fill his nights with me. I should have done the same, refused to let the world creep into my life. But I didn't. I coped. When the letterbox slammed I stopped rushing, I stopped crumbling, I stood straight and faced myself each morning, swallowing my fears, pushing away my anger with such force. I stopped staring at his picture, stuffed it to the bottom of a drawer and the bottom of my mind and would not let it resurface.

I inflated my life with trips to the shop, visits to his family, where his father would blink at my son, our son, as though he didn't recognise him, as though he was seeing someone else standing before him. My mother and I sewed together for hours, and I persuaded myself I was doing something productive, tricking my heart into believing I was useful.

And the days passed. They didn't fly by, the way joy often does, but passed, steadily, into yesterday, and I forgot him. I let James forget him a little too, let his image grow into a myth, so that the boy always thought of his father as a great hero, a little unreal, something untouchable. Perhaps I shouldn't have done that. It instilled in James an awe quite unbreakable, so that when Joseph finally returned, James did not know quite how to be with him, was not quite sure he deserved his father's love.

God, the things we do, the things we say. How meaningless after the event.

I was so angry at him when he came home. Not angry with him, just at him. Silly little mannerisms he had, they made me wonder why I hadn't noticed them before. The way he ate with his fork in his right hand. James would copy him, which frustrated me even more. Why did he want to be like the man he didn't know, the man he couldn't understand even if he read all the words in the world?

James, you must read Gulliver's Travels. I will ask you about it when I come home. I am like Gulliver...I am travelling the world and meeting giants that I will strike down with my mighty sword! Why didn't James copy me; the woman who had breathed life into the man he held in such high esteem? But how can you blame a child for loving a man who you have lifted high above the clouds?

After that war, without warning he returned and turned our lives upside down. Even when you know it's not always someone's fault you still blame them. I blamed him for the years of letters and loneliness. *You won't forget me will you? I will be home soon, I promise. Then we can be a family again.* They were filled with the words of a dying man, words that no young husband should ever know. Perhaps it was this knowledge that I resented so much. Knowledge I would never grasp, never share.

My selfish heart did not know how to recognise anything that wasn't normal. Suffering was unfamiliar to me. I refused to notice it as it sat by the window, looking out at a world it couldn't reach. I could not clear the clouds from his face. And I acted in such an unforgivable way as he settled back in. I tried to stop him from writing: tried to stop him from thinking of all he had seen, through eyes that could no longer cry. I wanted him to forget everything so that I could pretend I was not ignoring it.

It took me five weeks before I could read his first published piece. The words stabbed at me, opened my eyes to horrors I didn't want to see, forced me to smell death, innocence lost and see destruction splashed across the beautiful, clean pages. That poem tore at my heart. I thought I might die from my heart breaking, but breaking for the wrong reasons. Weeks of ignoring his words, ignoring him.

I had thought, before he left, that 'I love you' were magic words. Words that could erase mistakes and bring people back to life, three words that could say I'm sorry, I care, I know; all at once. But when he told me, heavy against my face at night and first thing as the morning winked at us, he didn't know. He cared, and he was sorry, so damn sorry, but he just didn't know. It wasn't his fault. And it wasn't mine. It wasn't my fault that I had forgotten him, forgotten how to speak.

Each night I turned away from him, my back holding no welcome, my cold manners such a torment to him. Why didn't I let him fall into me, take comfort in me and enjoy some warmth and some peace? I suppose I just didn't know how. I could see he was so tired of struggling, so confused by my anger.

'Why won't you let me love you Beth?' he had asked me one night, a couple of months after he had come home. I had pretended to be asleep.
I could not have stood it if he had begged me for an answer. I did not have one.

Chapter Eleven: Saturday

Beth, aged 84

It is Saturday, and as I wake up I think instantly of James. Not my son James, the little boy still lost within, but the charming man of yesterday. How like his brother he is, despite his wrinkles and crooked right front tooth. Joseph is forever young of course, but I can see through James' shell to the frame of his face beneath, and they are very alike.

I muse on these similarities as I swing out of bed and pull on my dressing gown. I can hear Peter, already up, whistling in the bathroom. For the first time since we arrived, I realise we have nothing to do. We are not visiting an old haunt, we are not going for a drive to Polperro or Looe. I am at a loss for a moment until I decide to walk up the hill to the White House and see James.

The sky is a bright blue as I open the door and step out. I am singing to myself as I climb the hill, slowly. I find I am a little excited to see James. Oh dear. When I reach the top of the hill I turn around and gaze out to Fowey. I can see the ferry chugging across the river. I can see a group of people huddled together on the quay, although I can't make out their faces, it is too far away.

I spin round again and continue up the hill, towards the house that began my tale. The house that began my life, really. As soon as I see it I notice the daffodils in the front garden, blinding, there are so many of them. I can smell them, and I drink in the taste of their scent in my throat before pushing the gate open and walking to the door. The red paint is flaking off in places, but the bell is the same old brass bell that was there when I left. I pull it and wait for what feels like an age before James opens the door. The surprise on his face soon becomes delight and he invites me in graciously, tucking his shirt in as he ushers me in. Into the White House, into the past.

The study. Books everywhere, covering every surface, littering a lot of the floor and even wedged ungracefully on the windowsill. He retreats to the kitchen to make tea and I wander about the room, feeling the stories beating under the dusty covers all around me. I wonder which books were Joseph's. He had hundreds when we were married, but I insisted he bring to our new home only what he couldn't bear to leave behind.

I realise now, as I stand here in this study, that he couldn't bear to leave any behind, but he did anyway, for me. Such a love, to resist words. So silly that I didn't know how wonderful books were when I was young, I was so ignorant of their power. I was also ignorant of just how much they meant to Joseph. What a silly little girl I was. Still am, really.

I take a seat when James returns, and we study each other as we chat about the daffodils. He has a gardener, a young lad from the village, who comes twice a week to tear up the weeds and water the flowers. He remembers that daffodils are my favourite flowers, and I blush involuntarily. How on earth could he know that?

I am amazed just how much he knows about me, or rather what he senses about me, as we continue to talk through the morning. It's as though he recognises me, as though he already understands me. I can only imagine that his parents must have told him about me when he was younger.

Laura May

As the day stretches out before us we chat and just enjoy each other's company, although I can detect some nervousness from James that I cannot quite place. And then he tells me. I don't know why I'm so shocked, why it hits me like a slap in the face. Of course someone had to have them I suppose. But I don't want to hear this, I don't want to know. I just never considered that I would have to face the thought of this.

James has the other letters. From Joseph. Not only addressed to James, but to their parents as well. He even has some that were intended for me, that either were mislaid or left in the house when I left it. He has thousands of them, sitting in drawers and hidden in gloom. They are here, now, in this very house, sharing the same air as me. They are waking up, I can feel them, they are stirring, they know I am here. Suddenly I am scared and James sees my fear, instantly regretting telling me.

He moves over to the chair beside me and places his hand on mine. My breathing is shallow, but I find his touch oddly comforting, and instead of pulling away from him I lean into him slightly, let my head touch against the rough material of his sweater, and he smells clean. I pull back sharply, remembering myself, and a look of confusion sweeps over his face before he masks it with concern.
'I'm sorry Beth, I wasn't sure whether to tell you at all. But I thought you might want to see them, I thought... I'm not sure what I th-th-thought.'
As soon as he begins to stutter I smile without even realising it. James is so like Joseph was, so eager to apologise for anything that isn't his fault.

It's OK, I'm OK, everything will be fine. I just need to remember to breathe and everything will be all right.

James relaxes a little and pats my hand affectionately. He is a kind man, so soft in his mannerisms, with no airs and graces hanging over his head. It is refreshing to meet someone who shares such a past but doesn't presume to know a future.

I collect my thoughts, or rather my feelings, quickly, and ask him to continue. There is surely a reason he has decided to tell me about the letters, and he soon reveals it. He has a letter for me.

I realise, without him saying another word, what it is. It is the letter that Joseph wrote the morning he drowned. I know it in my heart, and as I digest this I am so happy. James explains how they found it, in a drawer, when they cleared some furniture from our beautiful home. I must have already moved out. I can't believe that I had forgotten it. I must have instantly blocked it out as soon as I saw Joseph lying still. So still. Too still, my heart must have forgotten to beat at that moment, for it lay still as well.

Lord, can you hear me now. God, I'm scared, and I'm drowning in my own memories, and my words are tumbling over each other, and this is getting harder, and I can't breathe, I don't know how to let this seep through my skin into my heart. Lord, can you hear my heart breaking with each dawn. Your mouth, Joseph. Your sweet, silent mouth, I need it right now against me. I need to stop this beating.

James hands me a tissue, and I notice that I am crying. Quietly, shutting him out. He knows this, but he lets me cry. I can't seem to stop. I am standing looking down at Joseph again, hearing my son's cries in my head, smelling the salt and fish of the quay all over again.

Then, in this present moment, James leans down and kisses me gently on the cheek. He must be able to taste my tears now, I think absently. But it doesn't feel wrong, it feels good. Everything is going to be fine. He hands me a worn and wearied letter and I take it in between sobs, I clutch it like a life belt, let the paper graze against my fingers. I can feel Joseph's words coming alive beneath the thin envelope. They have been waiting for so long, waiting to be read and cherished as all words of love long to be.

I can't bring myself to read the letter now, not with James beside me, creating emotions within me that have been stilled for so long. I can't share this with him, with anyone and, as I slip the letter into my coat pocket beside my tissues and my sorrow, he nods. He knows, and he accepts. This is just what I need, and I am thankful for him in this moment. So thankful.

James stands, slowly, and I can see that age has crept into his bones the way it has crept into mine over the years. While he is in the kitchen, making strong coffee, I take the letter out again and look at the envelope, study it for any clue of what it may contain within its white walls. The seal is unbroken, nobody has read this letter. I am grateful for this; I don't want to share Joseph with anyone, even after all these years.

But there is no name on the front, he never wrote my name on the envelopes. He assumed that I would always find them myself, he didn't foresee someone else discovering his words. I wonder why James didn't open the envelope himself, to find out whom it was addressed to. Perhaps he just knew. I find as I sit in this comfortable chair surrounded by words that I like to believe this.

James returns to the study and I return the letter to my coat pocket. We drink the coffee in silence, neither of us wanting to break this spell, wanting to frighten away the ghost that has joined us here, in this room, in this house, in this village, where dreams are created with the morning and taken away with the setting of the sun. I am happy to have spent this day, but I must be getting back to the cottage, to Peter, to my life. I think for a moment, when I am standing at the door about to turn, that James might try to stop me, but he doesn't. He just leans into me, breathes me in, then shuts the door.

I find myself feeling sad as I descend the hill, feeling a fresh loss, as though I have known James for all my life, which in a way I suppose I have, without even realising it. I am impatient for this day to be over now, I am going to go back to the cottage, eat and then go to bed early. I am restless, tired of feeling and thinking all the time, never being able to switch off, never letting anything get away from me for long enough to forget it.

I am sick of forever contemplating impossibilities. I am tired, and I am old, and I need to stop. Stop thinking of things I can't change. I have learnt enough over the years to know I have learnt very little. I have seen enough to know I have seen only a small curve of the world and its wonders. I know I am old, I am aware that I will only grace this life for a few more years. I know this, and yet I am impatient to stop these thoughts and end the day in a peaceful sleep.

I wander down the hill and sit on a bench by the quay, looking at the river, at the place where Joseph lay the day they dragged him from her. Although I am impatient to go to sleep, I don't want to go back just yet and have to look at Peter's face. I look around me, taking in the sight of this quay, and I recognise that it doesn't hurt to be here. I am OK. It is not painful to see all these memories before me. It doesn't hurt any more. After all these years, finally it doesn't hurt any more. So I stand, slowly, and go back to the cottage. I'm ready.

Chapter Twelve: 1947

Beth, aged 26

My Beth,
Thank you for yesterday. It was a perfect day. The way
your hair wouldn't stay up in the scarf, that was perfect.
And the way it rained as soon as we left the warmth of
the house, that was perfect. So thank you. Each day we
spend together, each moment that we fill up in this
beautiful village with the eccentric characters that say
hello to us as we wander down the hill, is so perfect. I
don't think I will ever leave this place, it is too
enchanting, and you are here. We are here, together.
And we will grow old together here, wrapped in each
other's skin until we die, together, asleep in our bed.
And each day will be as perfect as yesterday.

It was a local dance. That's where I think I fell in love
with him again. It was being held in the village hall, and I
had spent the day baking and singing with James.
Thinking back, I wish something amazing and dramatic
had happened to throw us back into one another's arms,
but it didn't. I don't know why that evening proved any
different from all the others since he had come home,
but when I looked at him across the hall my breath
caught in my throat.

Perhaps it was because he looked so old, his coat a
little tattered, James so small at his side, clinging to his
leg. I can't remember what music was being played, I
can't remember what time it was, I can't remember what
I was wearing. In a moment he was all I could see. I had
practically run to him, pushing through the handsome
troops and hopeful girls, until I had his arm under my
hand. He had look so startled, as though my touch could
burn through to his skin. My mother's surprise was so

funny when I'd thrust James at her and dragged Joseph outside, into the cool night, into the hum of the sea singing all around us.

That kiss was the most amazing kiss of my life. So much more than my first kiss, or the kiss that created James, or our kiss goodbye on the morning he had left me. Joseph had been so nervous of kissing me back, so hesitant, needing such encouragement. It still makes me blush now to think of how desperate I had been that night to feel him inside me, how much I needed him to want me back. And the relief that had flooded through me as he kissed me back, the force behind his tongue and his teeth against my bottom lip and his hands urgently clutching at my dress as he'd pushed me up against the wall right there outside the village hall, against the darkness.

Suddenly all that mattered was our shadows dancing, my lipstick shining, his cold fingernail scratching at my face, my hair in our mouths as we struggled to sink deeper into each other. We could only tear our lips apart when we heard the young giggling of a couple a little way off. We giggled ourselves then, breaking the spell that had caught us in our kissing. He searched my face for a smile then, and I'd given it to him, knowing that we would be all right.

That night I let him into me like before, let him be gentle, let him breathe love back into me. When he whispered my name I sighed his own back, let him know that it was OK, that I wanted him as much as he wanted me. It must have been so awful for him, he had felt my indifference for so long, too long, my cold skin, my tight, forced smiles and politeness. I knew, throughout those years, that it wasn't his fault, that he had no control over

Fate, her cruel hand would take him away whenever she wanted, but still I couldn't love him.

That night, for the first time in years I actually felt it when he touched me, felt it when he brushed my skin with his lips. And it felt so good, tasted so right, smelt like love should, damp and sweaty and needy, desperate. He had made me moan, made me want again, let me sweep away all the tension I had caused him. He forgave me with his kisses, his rough hands pressing against me.

After, he sat up and smoked a cigarette. The smoke curled around our bodies as we lay in the dark, mingling with the smell of our passion, the taste of salt on our skin. I will always remember that night. I can never remember it on a page, not the way it really was or the way it felt, but I find I can hold onto the smell of him forever.

It had been so long. So long without any comfort or touch, years with only a vague routine tying us together. Of course we slept beside one another for those years, but we didn't wake each morning pressed against each other. We didn't open our eyes to each day with love for one another, or even lust, after a while. Thinking back, I'm not sure how we let it go on for so long. How had we slept at all during those years? How had we managed to smile for James? How had we dipped in and out of our lives at will, ignoring anything wrong?

We had circled one another like vultures ever since he had returned from that damned war, refusing to face anything that might tear us apart, picking at the carcass of our marriage. I can't explain what changed on that night at the village hall, what snapped. Perhaps I was just too tired and I needed someone, anyone, and

Joseph was all I'd ever known. Or perhaps I was finally over the fact that he had left me, perhaps I had finally forgiven him for fighting a war I didn't understand. Perhaps I had finally forgiven myself for not loving him when he came back.

We were like children again after that first night. Each day I loved a little more of Joseph, saw a little more of all I had ever wanted in him. I began to notice him for the first time in years, delighted in the sound of him mumbling to himself, recognised the love in his still eyes that had always been there, I just hadn't looked for it. And his letters began again. But they didn't cut me the way his letters had before, they didn't remind me that I couldn't calm the world.

The letters just made me smile again. *My Beth. You are mine again. I love knowing that, knowing you are mine. Thank you for letting me love you.* He began to smile again too, the words of war slowly being drawn out of him and onto paper, so that he could think of other things.

He wrote and wrote then, never stopping to eat, only stopping to kiss me and read to James, as though he could survive on kisses and words alone. My mother smiled now when she visited, instead of shaking her head when I told her Joseph was in the garden.
'I think your Letterbox Man has finally come home, Beth.'
'Yes, I think he has.'

Joseph began to annoy me again. I loved this. When he read in bed and turned the page down, I would be annoyed. When he muttered to himself in the garden, even after I had put James to bed, I would get annoyed. It was wonderful to actually notice him again, to react to him, even in a negative way. I had missed that so much, reacting to someone, acknowledging him in relation to myself.

When he first arrived home I was so numb, neither happy nor sad, just vacant. Nothing could rouse me to anger, could make me snap at him. He didn't seem worth my energy then. But we began to fall into each other again, to see what could be so wonderful about us again. I began to ache for the half light that would wake me in the morning to show me such a beautiful man beside me. I began to want him to go out, just so I could miss him, want him to come home. I forgot to be scared every time he left the house, forgot to fear he might not come home. I learnt to love everything about him again, the sound of him picking at his teeth, the feel of his skin when he came in from the cold and kissed me.

Joseph finally became a father after we fell in love again, too. He saw James, not as a child he could love too much, but as a little person, and he began to spend a lot more time with him. James grew so big, so loud, loving the sea just as Joseph did. This was something they shared without me. I would watch them, bobbing on the water in Joseph's small boat, and I would try to guess the secrets that they were telling each other, the whispers they were sharing. My two men, so precious, everything a woman could want.

They began to fill my days again, brightening them. Joseph began to be himself again, the nightmares eased a little, the doctor no longer spoke in hushed tones to me. He was mending, with my love, and I knew this was the reason he got out of bed each morning, got better, began to write again.

James held a light for him, as I did, and Joseph wrote little poems for him, wild fantasy stories to read to him at night, filling his young mind with wonders and love. Things got better. They got so good that I forgot Fate was singing in the background, whistling to herself as she gave and took without a care in the world.

And so it was that Fate arrived, cap in hand, begging. My first mistake, that day, was that I woke him. Gently, with my kisses, I woke him. If I had not stroked his hair and whispered his name to a new day perhaps he would have slept forever. But then there's a ghost of a chance he may have woken to the morning himself, without my caresses. Thinking back I can't remember much, though the day lost its promise somewhere between dawn and nightfall.

I didn't know the day would be any different, I didn't know my world would crash and shatter in my very hands. I didn't even know the moment that it happened, my heart didn't lurch, trying to clutch hold of him, my senses didn't tell me like they should have. I had no idea.

He left me a letter on my pillow, as he had grown used to doing recently, in his romantic way. I knew before reading it what it would hold, promises of forever and dripping words of love. I knew, but I loved his letters all the same. Each was a little different, offering something he hadn't offered before, a new thought or sentiment. It lay on his pillow beside me when I finally decided to open my eyes to the day. I turned it in my fingers, felt the fleshy softness of his envelope in my hands, and put it straight into my drawer, to save for a moment of silence when I could give it all my heart and savour it.

The day held a hope, and within a couple of hours that hope would be given breath and I would be allowed to tell the world. I was pregnant. I knew, could feel through my skin, feel the life that was growing within me, secretly, showing nothing of itself yet. But I knew. I had an appointment with the doctor that afternoon, and then I could announce our doing to the world – we had created a child! I couldn't wait to see the delight in my mother's eyes, the stunned joy Joseph was sure to try and hide as he fretted over money and bedrooms and all the things I was ignoring as I washed my body in the chilly air of the bathroom.

The house held no sounds, only the hum of the sea outside the window filtering in. Joseph and James had gone out, leaving me to daydream and dither and generally waste the moments in thought. How I wish, now, that I had woken with the dawn, held tightly onto my love, fiercely, protecting it from the world. How I wish with my whole heart that I had stolen another kiss, another moment in time with him, let him inside me, let him fill me. But I didn't. I let the day unfold, begin like any other. I let him go without even knowing it.

I met my mother straight after I had seen the doctor, and as we sat in the café sipping strong, sugary hot tea, she noticed the smile dancing in my eyes, knew without asking the reason.
'So?'
'Yes, I am.'
And her face had lit up like a candle, her wrinkled eyes had looked at me with wonder, and I knew she was happy for us. In the wake of a nightmare we had created a hope, everything was going to be OK, we would love until we could love no more, and this life was the proof that we were going to be all right.

This miracle proved that we had managed to find each other again, through the rubble of a darkness that I thought would never lift, we had managed to fall in love again and produce a life. I knew then that I was not going to break, I was not going to bend. I could love him, so fiercely, he would never need anything else. I was finally ready to let the past fall away, let the years he was away be forgiven, let him love me like only he knew how.

The day was so wrong. The sun was brilliant, giving his rays for the entire world to enjoy. The breeze sung merrily in the air, enjoying his warmth. It should have been so dark, the sky should have been enraged, crying for the unfairness of it all. But it wasn't.

Perhaps that's why I didn't know. The blue face of Heaven fooled me into thinking everything was good, the day would end well with strong arms holding me and smiles fading on my lips as I closed my eyes. I wish I could speak better, allow my eloquence to match my pain. But I am feathered by sentiments falling down on me, as I remember that day without really seeing the way it passed before my eyes, without really smelling the sea, without really hearing the screams ringing in my ears.

Of course we heard the screams before we saw anything. Even with them wailing up from the quay, I didn't guess what could be wrong with my world, I couldn't see what might be happening outside what I had created for me and the new life within me.

I remember seeing the fear in my mother's face. She knew, without seeing. She felt it before I even realised what was happening. How did she feel it stabbing at her when I was so ignorant? It is only looking back that I suspect she had always known, had seen my fate so long before I had.

She stood so quickly the table threw itself up with her, scattering our tea and littering crumbs on the floor of the quiet, clean café. I had to force me feet to follow her, had to stop myself sitting back down and finishing my tea, wrestling with the idea that something might be happening that I didn't want to know about. It didn't make any difference in the end anyway; I didn't see anything.

I didn't make it further than the corner before my mother swiftly turned on her heel and wrapped her arms around me, suffocating me with her grip, muffling the screams still echoing from the quay. It was only then, when the world became a little quieter and my mother was holding me tighter than she ever had, that I realised the screams were James'.

I wish I could say I fought my mother's embrace, struggled against her grip and ran straight to my son. But I didn't. I sagged, limp and fragile as a child myself in my mother's arms, unable to stand. She half dragged me to the café, where she seated me firmly on a hard chair and left me there, stunned, not even able to cry.

I didn't know what to cry for. My only fear was that James had been hurt, was still hurting, and I wasn't there. What would Joseph think of me, not even strong enough to look after James, let alone another child? He would be angry that I hadn't gone to James, angry that I had let my mother boss me into staying in the café while she dealt with whatever tragedy was making him scream down there.

Perhaps it would have been better if I'd known, beforehand. I could have made sure I was there, could have whispered into his ear 'I'm here' as his eyes closed. He would have liked that. Or it could have been so much worse, I might have screamed and cried all my tears, leaving nothing left over for the nights that would follow. I might have been unable to look into his eyes, bravely, as he had looked into the eyes of so many dying men.

But I didn't know, didn't expect Fate to be so cruel to him, to me, to give with one hand while taking away with the other. I didn't know, even when Mother returned to the café and placed a screaming child into my arms, even as I began to gently rock him against me and calm him, even as I looked back into her face, questioning, slightly bemused by everything that was hurrying about me.

It was only when she said it, that I saw everything in my mind.
'It's Joseph' she stammered into the air, as though that would explain everything. And it did. The room slowed down a little then. I became aware of James breathing against me, asleep with exhaustion. I saw the tea seeping into the tablecloth where we had spilled it earlier, and thought, oddly, that it would need to be washed. I saw the deep teak tones of James' hair, and the pale ghost fleeting across my mother's face, the colours of a bright day trapped in the small café.

That's when I knew. That's when I thrust James into her arms and ran, silently, too scared to utter anything that might make things real, to the quay, saw them lifting his body out of the water. Saw my life falling into the river, swallowed up in grief and pain. And heard my screams tearing from my throat, unnatural, baying to escape from my heart.

They tried, half-heartedly, to hold me back. But I tore at them, clawed my way through to him. And violently I fell beside him, crushing him with my kisses. Already his hair was drying in the sunshine, already he looked better. But he wasn't listening to my pleas, he was somewhere else, listening to other people's laughter.

I was screaming at him, while I kissed him, his skin slippery beneath my lips, his hands not clutching mine like they should. He just lay there, his smile broken by the blood seeping from his lower lip, his eyes closed against the sun's rays. I don't know how long I lay there, against his wet body, pressing bruises into his chest with my grasping hands, sobbing until my eyes blurred against all that was happening.

I fell asleep lying against him, trying to warm his skin with my kisses, whispering into his ear his own words, repeating to him the promises he had made to me, choking back the anger that kept rising like bile against my tongue. I fell asleep, for the last time, in his arms.

I remember somebody muttering, and I thought Joseph was in the garden, writing and muttering to himself again.
'Enough' he said, but his voice was old and gruff and I was hiccuping against his warm sweater as he lifted me into his arms. I felt like a doll in his arms, he was so strong, carrying me, protecting me with his safe arms and his smoky sweater. I remember thinking he smelt a little of the sea, and then I fell back to sleep before any more memories could ruin my dreams.

I don't remember Josh, one of the ferrymen, picking me up, untangling me from my dead husband, and carrying me home. I don't remember him smiling at me as he lay me down on my bed, our bed, and tucked the covers around me. I don't remember anything other than losing everything I ever needed. God only knows what happened that day. The sun forgot to hide its face with shame, the river forgot to love her lover. Joseph slipped away, and with him went my heart.

I can recall someone placing me against the smell of him, and I remember wrapping the sheets around me thinking he was holding me. But I don't remember the things I should. I don't remember what the doctor said to my mother outside the door in whispers, even though I was listening. I don't remember letting go of James when they brought him into me, but he wasn't there when I woke up. I don't remember the moment I lost everything.

Finally, the weather righted itself. The beautiful, bruised and darkened face of a storm leered down upon the village, its features casting an angry blackness, allowing me to be swallowed. I lay in bed for days, listening to the wind thumping against the windowpanes, the rain crying down from the furious heavens. Despite my mother's vain attempts to rouse me, I remained locked within my room, unable to stir. Our room. The room that breathed life into our first kiss, our first son, and also the life inside me. Our room, our sunny house. Filled with a love that I thought could withstand anything.

Whenever I ventured to the bathroom I would crumble upon the coarse, rough carpet on the landing and think, 'our stairs'. The stairs he had guided me up, tugging on my hand gently, the night of our wedding. The stairs he had taken two at a time to capture the first glimpse of his first son. The stairs he had once stumbled on, breaking a toe. I couldn't remember which toe, and suddenly this seemed so horrific to me, as though if I could only remember he would come back to me. A good wife would have known, I kept telling myself.

I hid in that bedroom, the cold creeping under the curtains and into my poor, broken heart, as I clung to the smell of him that lingered in the room. I pulled on the tatty old cardigan that he wore when he wrote, felt through the pockets like a thief, holding onto a broken pencil that I found there for days, as though it was all I had left of him.

I listened to the wind, and James whimpering against my mother's breast outside the door as he tried to gain admittance to my room, just to see me.
'I don't understand' he would whine. I could hear him clearly each day, but I buried my head under my husband's pillow and drowned his voice out. One day his voice would sound like Joseph's, I knew.

The problem was that I did not understand either. I did not understand why that day had begun like any other, deceiving me, lulling me into a false sense of security that I should have shaken free with all my might. I didn't understand why that morning had erupted in a blaze of glory like any other.

It is amazing what you miss. That first touch in the morning, brushing against you. The warm, fuzzy love that envelopes you as your eyes flutter open, and the only reason you know that the body entering yours is the right one is from that unexplainable recognition of the right pressure, the right breath against your ear, the right hands upon your throat. It felt, each of those first mornings, that my body was physically aching for him.

God, I ached.

I tried so hard to step aside from my sorrow, to let go of all my anger, but I couldn't do it immediately. Each morning I fell hard against the sheets in reality, the roar of his death stinging my face. Each day I would fall fast to denial, hug my skin against me and hope I wouldn't remember how he was the better half of me. Each day I wanted to think it would all be all right, but wanting something doesn't make it so.

What I couldn't grasp was that I had lost him, just when I'd finally found him again. I had lost so much, all of his warm smiles, all of his knowing looks, even all of his angry words whenever we argued. We would never argue again. I would never see the heat reach his face as he shouted at me, I would never more see his hands flying about in rage.

I had lost so much. He was the only one I couldn't pretend with. I tried sometimes; I tried so hard to pretend with him, to pretend I was OK when he left me to fight someone else's war, I tried to pretend I still loved him when he returned, I tried to pretend it didn't matter. But I couldn't pretend with him. I couldn't pretend to be all right when I began to fall into him again, fall in love with him over and over each time he smiled at me. I couldn't pretend that I didn't care any more.

He was the only one. The only person in my life who could look at me and see through me, who could hold me and make the world fade, who could sigh 'It's OK' into my ear and know I would believe him. He was the only one. How do you replace that? How do you fill your life up with other thoughts? How do you let go of the only thing that was decent and good and clean in your life? I just couldn't. I could not abandon my need to be with him, I needed to hold onto it tightly, so tightly, and never let it go.

I cannot really describe the pain I felt when Joseph drowned. It's hard to even remember it, the mind has a canny knack of shutting down in the face of such grief. For weeks I thought constantly of how he had drowned. He had never learnt to swim, like most people whose lives are entwined with the sea. Had he struggled, fought, gasping for breath? Had he seen my face, seen his son's face, swimming before him? Had he cried, softly? Had he been aware of all the moments he was losing by being caught in that one?

Like rapid waves my thoughts crashed against me. Had he known all the perfect moments he would no longer see? Had he floated away peacefully, knowing that it was just time? Asking these questions, over and over, was like a drum beating in my head, but I couldn't stop myself thinking about it. I wish I had just stopped thinking altogether, stopped the images merging in my mind. But I couldn't.

I wished, after time began to pass, that I hadn't reacted the way I did. I wish I hadn't hidden inside my heart, letting him engulf me, press against me until I couldn't breathe for wanting him. I wish I had shut down, become vacant and practical and uncaring in my response. But I didn't. I let it all wash over me, let the fact stare me in the face and let my body feel the full impact of his death slap and bruise me until I could cry no more.

However, things always change. I wish I could say I remained in our bedroom, letting my life slip away with my health holding its hand, but I did not. I eventually snapped, got up, got dressed, and felt the sharp selfish edge of my self-pity as I looked into my son's eyes. I finally needed to be again, to be a mother and a daughter and myself. I needed to climb out of my sorrow and let each day begin again.

The day I buried my husband, with my heart, it rained. I was thankful for that, it hid the tears of his beautiful mother and the pain of his brave father as they buried their first child. The rain soaked into my coat, edged its way under my skin, until my bones became cold. It should always rain when there is a funeral, I think. It is right, it is fitting. The day that Joseph was buried in the quiet, soft earth of the village church, the rain helped me. And as I walked home with my mother, clutching James' hand tightly, she had smiled at me. She knew that, eventually, it would be OK.

James helped so much. How dependent mothers become upon their children in times of crisis. I depended on James to light up whenever he saw a new toy, or to fall asleep soundly as I read to him each night. I needed that routine, his familiar responses, to keep me afloat. The sea of agony that ripped through my body each day was blocked whenever I heard him singing, sweetly, like sugar. Whenever he picked me a daffodil, whenever he smiled up at me for reassurance, whenever he cried and came to me for comfort, it helped.

I began to see a lot of Joseph in James, began to recognise all the little traits that I had somehow forgotten to notice over the years. The same flash that entered his eyes whenever he was frustrated, the same half smile that he would pull across his face whenever he had done something he shouldn't have.

And I began to feel the life inside me grow, as it started to stretch my clothes a little over its bump, and I realised I needed to smile again, if only so my baby could smile back at me when he was born. Perhaps I placed Joseph within James, perhaps I created similarities that weren't necessarily there. But it helped so much, and James grew into each similarity in time anyway.

In a lot of ways I was lucky. I could have lost the baby from shock, and I nearly did that day. But we were both healthy, despite my heart breaking. The Spencer family could have shunned me, but they did not. They held me closer to them than before, they wrapped me up and let me cry for longer than should have been allowed. And my mother remained constant, filled with a fresh sorrow, but constant.

And things got easier, though they shouldn't have. Eventually months passed, though I can't remember them passing. Days stretched out and my child snuggled against me, unaware, innocent. He would never meet his father. This was a tragedy more for me than for him. I wanted to see Joseph cradle his new son, I wanted to see the look of wonder on his face. But he would never meet this baby, not in this life.

And throughout this time of sorrow, the river flowed forever to the sea, unashamed, mocking my loss. It was the constant sigh of the river, the river that had once felt like home, that started to wear me down. It began to haunt me. I had loved that river, let her swallow my fears as a child and hug me to her as an adult, but I couldn't stay. No matter where you go in Polruan you can't escape the river. It follows you quietly everywhere, it softly invades your sleep, and its rhythm could, at times, be so comforting.

When Joseph was gone, it began to possess me, it was all I could think of. Every time I left the house my eyes would involuntarily be drawn to the river, and I would catch myself gazing at Fowey for hours, picking out nothing in particular, forgetting why I had left the house at all.

So we had to go. We had to get as far away from that river as possible. I needed a new river, one that hadn't swallowed the one man I would love forever. I needed to escape my past for a while.

The one thing I hated was leaving my mother. She yearned to see my Letterbox Man muttering to himself again almost as much as I did. She seemed to be grieving for all the men ever to be lost, ever to have fallen into the arms of Fate, the arms of the river, the sea and Destiny. But she didn't stop me from taking my beautiful boys far away from their rightful childhood, away from my pain.

And so I left, and lived my life. Without my Letterbox Man beside me, but holding onto him inside.

Chapter Thirteen: Sunday

Beth, aged 84

I sit on this bench, as old as me I imagine, if not older. I remember listening to my own mother as she became old. Older and wiser, wrinkled and even more beautiful. I am old myself now. I am a little wiser, I hope, and I am definitely more wrinkled. I am also more beautiful. My thoughts are of beautiful places, beautiful sounds and faces. And I am sitting here on this bench, looking out on my past, into the ocean.

I remember sitting here with Kitty as a child, looking out at the wonder of the sea before us and dreaming of one day having our own fisherman to worry over and fret about. I remember sitting here with Joseph, only once though. He brought me here to propose. Our peak, he called it afterwards. We could see his house from here, and I look over at it now, remembering.

That day was blustery and bold, whipping around us as we giggled and stumbled up here, our faces fresh. I knew he was going to propose that morning when I had skipped downstairs and seen the light fluttering in my mother's eyes. He had obviously already asked her permission, and I could see a glimmer of sorrow shadowing her face as she smiled at me. As we sat and ate breakfast I think we were both silently missing my father.

Funny to think of it now, but I can't remember what I ate that morning, the morning Joseph proposed. But even without my mother's delight shining from her like a beacon, I knew he was going to propose, in my heart. He had held my hand so lightly as we climbed the hill, as though he was afraid to crush it. I remember it so well, although obviously the memory is coloured with layers of the happy moments that I later shared with him. The wind had made my eyes sting. And I remember I cried, like the child I was, at the prospect of being forever loved, forever protected.

The wind is whipping at my grey hair now, and I can feel him kissing me as I look back through time at that day, fondly, without any sadness left inside me to taint it. I recognise the impatience that is sitting inside me at the moment. I'm impatient now, to be with him again. It has been too long. It has been a lifetime.

I feel like such a cliché, sitting here on my peak, with grey hair and old hands and a heart full of memories. But I'm a happy cliché. The sea is calm today, despite the wind, and I imagine what it would feel like to sink into it, let it wash over me, cold and comforting. I should be getting back, Peter will be worrying.

I think of the day Joseph proposed. How young we both were, how full of hope. I remember he had stuttered, in his charming way. All the confidence of education and breeding cannot stifle the nerves of young love.
'My Beth, will y-y-y-you marry m-m-me?'
I hadn't even answered. I couldn't speak. My throat had tightened, and I could only nod my acceptance.

I let the tears stream silently down my cheeks as he lifted me up, twirled me around, caught me in his love. He was always such a nervous man, always so unsure of himself in my presence. I still find it hard to understand this. I think that, now, this is the reason great love survives. The willingness to accept that you can't understand everything. The ability to simply accept someone without question, and love them for it.

I remember, sharply, abruptly, a gift that Joseph gave me after we got engaged. It was a pair of pearl earrings. I remember it now because I want to wear them, but I can't think where they might be. That was one of the great things about Joseph. He never bought me gifts that I needed. He always bought me something beautiful, something I wanted.

So impractical, so unnecessary. So beautiful. He always surrounded me with beauty, preferring to buy me flowers than cutlery, buy books rather than pay bills. I never appreciated this quality in him then, I didn't understand it. I still don't understand it I suppose, but I do appreciate it now.

This place is amazing, I realise as I sit here, an old woman with her old love. When I consider the thousands of faces that haven't seen this sight, I feel sorry for the world. I feel sorry for my boys, for all I denied them, this magical world of wonder that can reach into you and tear out any doubts or worries.

I regret many things in my life. I regret taking my boys away from their inheritance, all the beautiful days here. I regret not letting anyone else into my heart after Joseph died. I regret that I never met someone, anyone, who could look after me now in my old age. Someone to relieve the burden from my children. But for each regret I have had many moments of happiness in my life, and for that I will never be sorry. I have been so lucky in my life.

Some people never meet their other half, the half that completes them, that fits. For losing Joseph, I will never regret that I found him first. Nobody can regret all that made them happy and whole, regardless of pain and loss. It is difficult to think of Joseph without missing him, but I am lucky to have someone to think of at all, and I am lucky to be here, sitting on this peak, watching the day fade.

I'm glad now, as I sit on this weary bench, that he proposed to me here. It is where my heart lies. I'm happy he wasn't a romantic man, wasn't prone to whimsical displays of affection, that he held his heart next to mine and never thought to test our love. He didn't need to prove he loved me. He just knew it, as he just knew that he had to propose here, while we were alone with the sea and the air.

At the time I remember thinking it would have been wonderful to propose when everyone we knew was with us, so that they could share our joy. But now I am glad that only I own this memory. It is mine, nobody else invades it, I think of nothing but him and me, here, alone.

The ring was so stunning, it glittered and gleamed like all things beautiful should. He didn't give me the ring until he had asked me. He gave me his words first, as he always did, let me take in his love, feel it like thunder in my heart, before he brought the ring out into the light. It was a gold band with a tiny diamond set in the centre. It was the most extravagant thing I had ever seen. I had heard of great riches, but never tasted them.

In that moment I felt I would have married him regardless of love, purely for that exquisite ring. Now I am old, and I know that I never would have married him without the deepest love, but that morning, the brightness and wind lashing at us with excitement, it was intoxicating. I felt like water, free and forever moving in the right direction, following my fate. Strange, to think that being so bound, forever, to another person would create such a sense of freedom, of liberty. I was at liberty to love then, so young and ready to love. I miss that freedom now I am old. I miss the love that I once owned, the love that was mine to give.

I understand, as I stare out from this peak, that even now I still mourn him. But God only knows what I'd have been without him. I'd never have moved out into the sunlight. I'd have missed out on a life. If his fate had never brushed against mine I would not have my two beautiful boys, the wrinkles of a thousand smiles lining my eyes, or so many memories littering my mind.

I dip my hand into my coat pocket and lift out, gently, the tattered letter that he had written on that fateful morning. Still, I haven't let my eyes caress the words. I just couldn't bring myself to look at it. It's the last letter he ever wrote to me. Perhaps I hoped that one day the letterbox would once again slam for me. But now it is time.

I'm ready. So much time has passed, so many new moments have beaten against me, I need to read the letter here, now, or I never will. The envelope is so worn by time, by my fingers pushing against it over and over again in the last few hours, trying to guess the words since James gave it to me, but never daring to tear the seal.

Perhaps, even if I had had the letter all these years, I just never possessed the courage before. But I'm strong now, old and tired, but still strong. I take one last look at the sea, its greys and blues and greens painting themselves out among the waves just for me, just for this moment. The wind calms, holds its breath with anticipation. It seems as though the sea, the wind, the very Earth have also been waiting for this moment, for this release. I finally break into the letter, and steal his last words.

My Beth,

Just a little note to say I love you. So simple, but I cannot seem to tell you enough. I know I am very demanding…I demand a smile from you every day for the rest of your life, a smile just for me, that creeps into the corner of your mouth and spreads across your lips like a dancing kiss. They are my favourite smiles, and you do them so well. You smile like that when James stumbles over his words as he reads to you every night…I confess I have watched you many times. You smile like that whenever a new daffodil breaks free from the Earth in the garden as well. You smile like that when I whisper in your ear…even though I cannot see your face I can feel the smile through my own lips on your skin.

I don't think I could ever go away again, and leave that smile. I would miss it even more than the last time I went away, I would miss the infectious shape of it that catches everyone who sees you. I love your smile.
Joseph x

I read the letter quickly, eager, hungry for each word, hungry for him. I become aware that I'm holding my breath, and I let it out slowly. I read it again, slowly, letting the syllables wash around in my mind and travel gradually to my heart. I realise I was expecting some kind of goodbye, perhaps an amazing revelation. But of course he doesn't say goodbye. And in a way he didn't need to; he never left me.

I let a smile begin on my lips, one of the smiles he loved so much, and I let my eyes leave the page, his scribbled, rushed words, and I gaze out at our world around me. Eventually I prise my fingers from the old paper, put it back in the envelope, and place it safely in my pocket, beside my love. I stand up, my old bones creaking with the effort, and drink in the view for a few more seconds.

Enough, I think.

It is time to go home.